Allen of Kea

AOK

James Hawkins Woodward

Integrity

AUTHENTIC IDEAS

ISBN (Paperback): 978-1-7396740-7-6

A copy of the CIP report for this book is available from the British Library.

Authentic Ideas is an imprint of Integrity Media Ltd, a UK publishing company.
www.integrity-media.co.uk

Printed and bound in Great Britain by Clays Ltd, Elcograf S.p.A

NOTES FROM THE PUBLISHER

Integrity Media is a publishing company focused on helping individuals who are dealing, or have dealt, with poor mental health to tell their stories. In doing so, we enable our authors to move forward and our readers to better understand the challenges of mental wellbeing for their own education and support. Therefore, books published by Integrity Media, including this one, contain mature themes, frequently relayed in an open and honest manner. The content we publish remains approved and safe, but we believe that each of us may react differently. To enable you to decide if this work may be suitable and/or appropriate for you, we provide a list of the themes contained in this publication.

The following topics are mentioned in this book:
Addiction (drugs, alcoholism and others)
Sex and sexualisation

Warning: This book features further explicit content such as swearing and other vulgar language, illustrated imagery of body parts, and local dialects.

If you, or someone you know, are struggling, go to

https://www.integrity-media.co.uk/support/

for more information on how to take the matter into your own hands and find a helpline.

NOTES FROM THE AUTHOR

An apology seems a fine place to commence any dialogue, whether it be fact, fiction or a vague mix of both. AOK is this, an endeavour to skate across the thin ice that is the complexity of human condition. It is a comedy; it is a tragedy; yet, sincerely, it is neither. It is fundamentally a testament to reinvention, love and encouragement to those of us who bear witness or experience the pain, fear, insecurity and utter despair that is depression. It is a tool to use with might and valour against those three am vicious demons of a new day. Seek out a dictionary and turn to the D words, note their vast negative meanings, inflections and purpose, no other letter holds this dread. Yet it sits and waits like a vulture after C. Humour is often a way to combat or hide behind this condition. The words I use, maybe, and hopefully so, are vulgar and politically incorrect. However, they are important, their past established in antiquity. They should not be edited out with asterisks as popular culture, or more often than not unpopular, dictates. We cannot reinvent the wheel. This book is meant to bring joy, hope and happiness in bleak times. AOK is no harbinger of doubt to anyone's religious beliefs, sexual preferences, race, nationality, creed or colour. For theologians, classicist of Greco-Roman and Ottoman culture, I freely admit that certain liberties have been taken. I confirm that names and references are fabricated and only mentioned in the name of comedy and certainly not meant to cause any offence. AOK is my attempt to make tomorrow a better day. A day of peace, love and understanding for all.

For Amanda and Zeus
The Poet lives on in all of us somewhere

During my last visit to my psychiatrist, I was handed a wooden apple and asked if I would peel it. I turned it in my hands, felt its unblemished surface and replied, 'I'll peel it, if you eat it.'

Amanda J Woodward

Prologue

The good Doctor advised a radical career change, a new life, a fresh start somewhere warm and certainly not the existing, tedious Line Manager position at Toyota Motor Manufacturing plant. All remains battleship grey there, the fortress, made in Japan, but part of Burnaston, just off the A38 before Derby.

'How about travel or something?' Suggested the Doctor. 'Something to let your mind expand and escape the mediocrity of our humdrum existence.'

Here, Allen seriously questioned whether it was he who needed intervention and not the Doctor. But the travel thing made sense. With no family, few friends and nothing to stop him. Just refresh the CV with some more lies, add that he is fluent in Greek and Italian—which he is not—use the usual bullshit at the interview and here he is now, on the Greek island of Kea, the pearl of the Aegean Sea.

1
Allen

Allen Mason Freeman, not the Alan "Fluff" Freeman of British radio fame in the sixties, seventies, and eighties, but Allen Mason Freeman, the reborn tour representative extraordinaire for Laskarina Holidays. The homes are of the famed Greek flag, beautiful blue and white colours, "Η Γαλανόλευκη" (I Galanolefki), the azure and the white, "Η Κυανόλευκη" (I Kyanolefki). A marvellous flag, almost as good as the Union Jack in design. Allen Mason Freeman. *Wish I was,* thought Allen, *a freeman*. From this present home, a flat above the local bakery, he trudged out into the early hours, his hangover not helped by the already warm August morning.

Kea, known locally as Tzia, is a remote Greek island basking in the Aegean Sea's Cyclades. The archipelago is Allen's main operating area, although the other island he is in charge of, Sifnos, does occasionally include a couple of villas. Allen prefers Kea. He likes his small balconied apartment and the smell of freshly baked bread that permeates from below. His tour remit, as every professional holiday representative knows, is to look after his guests, their every whim and wish catered for. The reality, however, is somewhat different. Firstly, as do the locals, he hates the tourists who visit to spend their drachmas and leave like broken red lobsters.

Allen's coping strategy is to stay out of their way as much as possible, try to have a life and work on his tan. He already looked like a piece of stretched russet leather with creases. He sets his mobile phone to permanent automatic answer, ignores his messages, and politely assists the usually-complaining British punters who disembark with alarming regularity, from the yellow Flying Dolphin ferry that departs from the port of Lavrion, near Athens.

Allen is a man of the classics, hence his interest in Greco-Roman mythology and history. But he is also a classic depressive. If his condition could be categorised, it would be somewhere in grade one. Which is why his doctor's advice regarding his radical career change at fifty-two has been so important to stabilise his mental health issues. That, alongside the Ouzo and regular sunshine to boost his serotonin levels and vitamin D. Allen is on various medicines for his brain and blood pressure, although the latter is, in fact, worse than his brain box.

Allen reads much and is keenly interested in amateur archaeology, an interest that has actually caused his arrest, but without charge, for an attempted dig he decided to perform in a part of an old temple located in a truly inaccessible place off an isolated beach on the island. This expedition involved one fluorescent pink Lilo air bed, a small spade, and a dangerous crossing for the offshore clump of soil and rock adjacent to the beach; the reputed burial site of long-dead pirates who were buried with gold or silver coins on their eyes, the choice of metal he assumed depending on how good a pirate they had been.

Allen likes women, although he does have difficulty remembering the last important date he has been on, and how long ago a seriously needed shag had occurred. *Still,* he thought, *plenty of time yet. At least no Japanese early-morning training session at Toyota on the A38.* It was never a clever idea exercising on a busy dual carriageway.

Allen plays the bouzouki, the four-stringed version of the mandolin also known as tetrachordo. Oddly, he plays it but much better than the three-stringed one. This talent he uses on the Greek-themed music nights to entertain the tourists that bother to turn up. Mostly, it is those that ain't already off their tits on Ouzo or Retsina, an acquired taste at the best of times, unlike the local Raki fire water. That stuff could strip paint off a door at thirty paces. Allen reckons Raki is the real reason that the Greeks and Turks fell out all those years ago. A) they both liked it and still do; B) they drink too much of the stuff; and C) which of the proud nations has actually invented it remains a question—that and kebab, of course.

Allen is a keen and skilled cook. He can make the best stuffed eggplant dolmades, and goat stifado, an unlikely dish for a man with occasional late forties to early fifties erectile dysfunction. His stew is legendary though, and possibly better than the locals'. For his age,

Allen is trim and has hair, which successfully knocks off eight years. Coincidentally the same length of time he has worked for Laskarina, which has now sadly closed. But although his body remains toned, his brain is fucked, his blood pressure awful, and yet his life expectations remain high. He writes music on a Yamaha-DX7 keyboard that he brought with him from the UK in his old, stickered flight case.

Allen is vaguely cool in an eccentric kind of way, handsome with a not-too-lined face that tells stories as good as he does in conversation. Theoretically, he should be popular with the ladies, but he misinterprets, or simply doesn't notice, mild flirtation. In truth, a more direct approach is needed to attract his attention. Throwing panties at his face springs to mind. However, this has never happened!

He loves Kea; he loves his bakery flat; he tolerates the tourists, as do his Greek friends. He is an active, strong swimmer, and for all his faults, his part-time girlfriend Penelope, who lives in Athens, cares about him. However, she hasn't told him so. The last time they were together was over nine months ago.

2
The guests

Allen closes the paint-stripped and largely faded ocean blue door of his flat. There was no point in locking it, there was no crime on the island and nothing worth stealing inside. *Who needs Ikea when you've already got crap gear!* Allen sets off to the main port of Korissia in the bay of Saint Nikolaos. Now we are not talking Dover or even Le Havre. Korissia is small and quaint with tavernas and fairy lights pinned to half-painted olive trees. He looks at his schedule documenting the new arrivals. Grace and Christian Houseman-Smith, their name stands out, probably the double fucking barrelled surname. *This is going to be fun*, he thinks, already visualising images of the couple. Or maybe not, the fun part that is.

Grace and Christian Houseman-Smith are the first to walk down the ramp from the yellow Flying Dolphin ferry. To Allen, initial impressions are always important. He instantly notices the matching Louis Vuitton travel luggage with cloned side shoulder bags. Allen notices that Grace has been sick as traces of the in-flight meal to Athens remain in her dyed blonde hair and slightly down her Chanel blouse. She wears what appears to be a ridiculously-uncomfortable pair of high white wedge-heeled sandals, in which she totters through sickness or too many gin and tonics. Either that or the dolphin hasn't been flying right. *Good job it's yellow*, he thinks. Shame for the stained Vuitton though. Grace looks like she is in her mid-forties, but with a severe teen attitude.

'This is mother of God awful!' She screams at Allen by way of introduction. Allen waves his welcome to Sicknos—*sorry, poor taste that one, literally*. He waves his welcome to Kea, Laskarina Holidays clipboard tilted in their direction.

'Get me a bath right now, and a valet, and some stuff for diarrhoea...'

The list is endless, so Allen gives up writing. Christian lights up a large cigar, too large for Kea. Grace coughs, as all non-smokers outside do.

'Right! Let's get you home then. However, I do have another couple from Bristol and a gentleman in a wheelchair to collect.'

'Fuck them,' counters Grace in an Essex accent, 'I don't give a monkey's ass!'

'Nooooo,' replies Allen, 'I can't do that.' He knows he can't do that in any department, not because of his occasional erectile dysfunction, but his terms of contract simply do not allow him to either leave them or fuck them.

He observes two young lovers struggling with two huge red and blue, logoed rucksacks, and bottled water. The woman is so hot in the looks department, so was the guy she was with. Allen would breach his contract for her, not him though. *Bet he's got a degree in something outstanding alongside being an Adonis, the bastard.* They see the Laskarina sign and wander over from the Flying Dolphin's disembarkation ramp, dragging their rucksacks. Allen looks at his list and holds out his hand.

'You must be Saffy-with-a-Y and Kevin-with-an-N.' *No one's perfect,* thinks Allen. Then he asks, 'Have you seen an old boy in a wheelchair and a gardener from Derbyshire South?'

They both shake their heads in unison whilst Allen considers how he is going to get the Louis Vuitton, Saffy, Kevin, the rucksacks, the wheelchair, the sick Grace, the cigar-smoking Christian, the Gardener and the Old Boy—that he has just spotted—into the very tight transit van. The man in the wheelchair, whom he has just observed being helped off, or more accurately thrown off the Dolphin in his chair, appears to be asleep. Or so he hopes. Allen acknowledges the white-uniformed flying boat helpers who ignore him and push the wheel-chaired, brandy-flask-holding and mildly snoring, elderly gent back to his flock. The ferry departs with no sign of the Gardener. The ill-matched group make their way to the waiting transit and silence and sanity return to the island, albeit temporarily.

The big-breasted and truly glorious Saffy sits next to the sack of sick Grace. Smoking Christian eases in up front; the old boy in the wheelchair, called Anthony, who turns out to be a poet, is belted at the back with the help of a muscled Kevin. He is parked with the sick Vuitton, Anthony's all leather, monogrammed valise—probably crammed with scotch—, and the rucksacks. Allen notices the poet's name is equally engraved on the flask nestling in his lap like a small hot water bottle should.

Anthony, grudgingly awake now, doesn't appear to give a toss. He takes another swig from it and shouts, 'Take me to paradise driver, and *Efharisto* (thank you).'

Wise men say nothing, thinks Allen, remembering a great line from some obscure punk band he used to play drums for.

'What's your bleeding name?' Asks Grace to Allen, not so politely and way too loud for the already sick-smelling confined space of the transit.

'Allen.'

'Well, Alleeeeeen,' she literally screeches his name, 'drop us off first, I'm gonna puke again. Do you have anything for sickness?'

'Not on me, sorry.' He thinks a sawn-off shotgun would be a useful medical treatment. 'But leave it with me. Not the sick!' He adds quickly, remembering all the occasions he has had to mop the van because somebody had been sick.

However, it remains his call and he does decide despite the detour to drop Grace and Christian how-fucking-pleasant-Houseman-Smith off first as he knows these two fuckers are going to be hard work. They pass Dimitri's famous fish taverna.

'Ideal for lobster!' Allen points out.

Grace retches and a big-breasted Saffy looks worried. Allen wonders if they are real, not the lobsters but Saffron's bouzoukis, apparently from Gloucester and not Bristol after all. Anthony, with the faulty brakes that Allen has previously tested on the road, rocks gently from side to side in the limited space, fast asleep on planet Whatever, but alive at least. Kevin the Wonderful is grooming his dark hair and throwing some muscle poses in his white figure hugging t-shirt, not Tommy-Hilfiger hugging.

3
The Villas

The first destination is the Villa Bougainvillea, aptly named for the purple and pink flowers on the terrace arbour, adjacent to the crystal aqua of the kidney-shaped pool with a 'Strictly no diving' sign.

Saffy opens the sliding door of the transit. First to get out, second, to inhale some fresh, uncontaminated air, free from Grace's heady perfume laced with an unattractive hint of puke. Kevin, still flexing his muscles, proceeds to the transit's rear door with smoking Christian, who wakes the sleeping Anthony by dropping a piece of Vuitton hand luggage on the poet's head. Anthony just grunts, still slightly in the grips of the brandy.

'Sorry old boy!' Christian apologises, flicking a large glob of cigar ash on the poet's flip flops.

Allen starts subconsciously humming, '"*I'm just mad about Saffron, wonder if she's mad about me*"'. Saffy ignores him completely, Kevin briefly, Anthony absolutely, and for the How-How-How-Fucking-Ill-Mannered-Housemans, obviously. Instead, she chooses to stare goddess-like at the not-too-distant aquamarine waters of the Aegean Sea.

The Villa Bougainvillea wears a huge rambling plant. It is clearly old but healthy, unlike the poet, and twists in a glory of pink and purple knots that adorn the entire frontage of the villa. There are also two ancient olive trees painted white in broad four-foot-high bands around the base of their ancient girths. Allen considers his aged girth and Saffy's truly fabulous and beautifully rounded ass in tight denim shorts. *Calm it*, thinks Allen. Perhaps Kevin will pull a muscle in his brain, which is obviously somewhere else, judging by the way he is chucking the luggage about. Either that, or in a previous job, he was an airline baggage handler. The couple is here for two weeks, at the next, slightly less auspicious, villa, the Hibiscus. The Villa Hibiscus also has olive trees, less ancient than at the Villa Bougainvillea, but then most country properties do. However, it is strange to note that

Allen has never seen a Villa called Villa Olive in all his Greek travels. Too Popeye probably.

The effervescent Grace, after demanding Allen's number, which he presents rather grandly on one of his Laskarina cards, totters off into the Villa in her ridiculous footwear someone would presumably only wear on a catwalk.

'The key is under the small white terracotta pot to the left side of the terrace door,' he shouts, 'not the huge pots, the small pot!'

Grace promptly moves one of the big ones, which have stood perfectly still since the dawn of time. It falls from the flag-stoned step and crashes onto the equally flag-stoned terrace. A fantastic piece of history shattered into a thousand pieces in two seconds…

'Oops!' Says Grace loudly. 'Soz, Alleeeeen! Get some fucker to clean up this mess!'

She finds the key to the large white double doors under the small white pot and lets herself in.

Yes bossa, Allen considers shouting after her but doesn't. Cigarman Christian adds, rather unhelpfully, 'Well, at least it wasn't new and the other ones are okay.'

And there you have it: Essex meets culture and Essex wins. *Just hope they don't plan a visit to the local Monastery of Panagia Kastriani.* Christ knows, and He probably already does, what would happen there.

Allen watches Saffron's beautiful butt cheeks wrapped in faded denim bounce along the path to the front door of the Villa Hibiscus. She is struggling with the two giant rucksacks that seem very heavy. *I wonder what the fuck they've got in there?* Bondage gear, Kevin's weights, the odd strap on … Perhaps a substitute for his small penis, the guy can't be that perfect.

Unlike the Houseman-Smiths, Saffy and Kevin don't break the pots to find their key. Allen has made a call to Nikos, his friend, to sort out the Houseman's pot, which caused slight confusion in the 'drugs versus terracotta' department. Allen prefers the Villa Hibiscus. He regards it as more intimate somehow. It has fewer rooms, simple yet tastefully furnished in traditional Greek style, and a vintage four-poster bed with full virginal white mosquito netting. A heady thought indeed as he imagines the glorious Saffy in an interestingly less goddess-like pose. *I must contact Penelope in Athens.*

'Thanks Allen', Saffron says at the door. "Now please go, we've got the welcome hamper to get through and some other business to attend to."

Allen notes a slight twinkle in her eye but understands deep down it is no twinkle for him. He breathes in the enthused, sweet-scented cypress air and listens to the cicadas' mating call. *Kevin, you lucky bastard.*

'Four down and one to go!' Says Allen aloud to himself, desperately hoping that he remembered to shut the door of the transit after the retrieval of the rucksacks.

The rear door is facing down-hill, and Allen is sure Anthony is still fast asleep in the chair without functioning brakes. He quickens his pace. He is immensely neurotic, worrying about the slightest thing. In fact, he worries about worry itself. He even worries if he is not worried which, really, is never. Thankfully, the transit's rear door is shut, and the poet sleeps still. Allen gets confirmation he is alive by the slight trace of spittle oozing from his mouth that pleasantly congeals with the warm air on his semi Salvador Dali moustache. His weather-beaten and once-white Panama hat now sporting the colours of his Crown Green Bowling association leans at a comical angle on his head.

Allen fires up the van. 'Villa Catriona is next. It is a charming, small one-bed apartment directly facing the sea front and right next to Mateo's Windy Bar, a favourite haunt of mine. Is everyone okay?' Allen shouts. He receives no response but a twitch from Anthony's moustache.

Apparently "Mateo" means "devoted to God", an unlikely name for a taverna situated adjacent to a small, decommissioned, white orthodox chapel that Mateo uses as storeroom. Yet equally unlikely given Mateo's rather dubious record as a seducer of permissible women. His most current tourist conquest was an over-eager septuagenarian woman who seriously enjoyed his companionship, advances, and certainly his gin and Italian cocktails, which he accompanied with a couple of Maraschino cherries. The Windy Bar, aptly named as it juts out on a promontory which catches the Meltemi breeze, in all its glory, during mid-May to mid-September.

That will certainly disguise Anthony's farts, thinks Allen catching another airborne waft that's complemented his drive back along the dirt road to the Villa Catriona. The villa should suit Anthony just fine. Next to Mateo's for food and by the look of things drink, all on one level with no steps, perfect for a wheelchair and easy access to the small beach. Allen pulls up to the Villa just as Anthony wakes up.

'You ok?' Asks Allen.

'Just peachy, dear boy, where's the bar?'

'Don't you want to see your Villa first?'

'Not really,' replies Anthony, 'more in need of some liquid refreshment, if you understand my groove. A vast quantity of Ouzo, my pen, and my pad.' He takes in his surroundings. 'A tad blowy here but very splendid, very splendid indeed, and so close to the water. I bet one can feed the fish from the bathroom. They like bread, you know. But unlike baby Jesus, not the wine and certainly not Ouzo, with or without ice. I wrote a poem about ice once, want to hear it?'

Before waiting for Allen's response, he launches into his poem.

Ice

Let the cold come home son,
let the cold come home.
Feel its icy hand son,
feel it chill the bone.
Watch it stop the river son,
watch it stem the flow—

Allen's phone rings. It's Grace. He rolls his eyes.

'Sorry Anthony, how rude of me. Please go on, this is good stuff.' He turns the phone to mute.

...
See its frosty gaze son,
see it through the snow.
Hear the word it whispers son,
hear its secret song.
Follow the path it makes son,

follow it along—

Allen feels the phone vibrate in his Bermuda shorts. *Fuck off*, he thinks, *this guy is good!*

...
the frozen road of winter son,
the road back to our door.
The place where you were born son,
before that bullet tore,
a hole deep in your dear chest son,
in their bastard war.

The applause coming from behind Allen surprises him. It is Mateo, whose knowledge of the English language, no doubt through his experience as a Casanova, is excellent.

'You have a fan, well, two actually!' Allen compliments him, shaking the Poet's somewhat sweaty hand. 'You are a good man and a cool poet.' He means it. 'What do you think, Mateo?'

'I think for that masterwork a large on-the-house Ouzo with ice is in order! Leave him and the key with me Allen. I will attend to you, Anthony, feed you and settle you in next door.'

'Promise?'

'I promise my word as a stout,' replies Mateo, getting the English saying slightly off, or maybe not for a taverna owner.

4
Scorpions

'Alleeeeen, there's a bastard scorpion in the shower bath thingy!'

Well, this is Greece, Allen thinks as he listens to the rest of the message.

'It's fuckin huge…'

What, Christian's cock?

'…The scorpion is gigantic and I need a baff!'

Obviously. Allen watches Mateo push Anthony to a beautiful table below the white awning fluttering gently.

'I smell of sick…'

So pleased you realised that.

'…please Allen, please help, you fucker, please!'

Allen assumes the *fucker* reference is a term of endearment and ignores it. *Can't you get Christian to hit the thing on its poor small head with your huge white sandals or has he already drowned in the pool?* Allen can't text this, though. Instead, he rings Hydra Grace. She answers immediately.

'Sorry, poor signal.' Allen makes some vocal fizz sounds.

'Where the pissing 'ell you been?' Grace enquires with her usual etiquette.

'Attending to my guests,' replies Allen.

'Well attend to me now will ya!'

'Where's Christian?'

'The fucker is slobbed out on a reclining white and blue sunbed by the pool with the welcome hamper wine, I think he's asleep.'

'Okay Grace … Do you mind if I call you that?' He asks out of respect.

'Yes I do! Call me Mrs Houseman-Smith with an *H*!' She spits.

'Okay H.' Allen replies, tongue in cheek. 'I'll be round in a bit. Find your sandals, I may need them.'

Allen hangs up. *Fuck her, the complete cow.*

Allen hauls himself back in the van. It is so stiflingly hot that he knows the drive back to the Villa Bougainvillea will be uncomfortable. Even with the windows down, which does nothing to alleviate the humidity, the dust that is shaken during the drive makes it more difficult for Allen to breathe. *Great. Twenty more minutes of this shit to fight a scorpion.* Allen wonders if his contract stipulates legal redress if he develops COPD, that is Chronic Obstructive Pulmonary Disease, from the dust roads or scorpion poisoning. He arrives at the Bougainvillea and notices that the busted pot has still not been cleaned up by Nikos.

'Fuck, that bastard hurts! Fuck.' Allen screams. He bends down and removes a very sharp piece of pottery from his right foot his sandal failed to protect. Just then, Grace, How-How-Perfectly-Badly-Timed-Houseman, opens the front door to greet him, clad in a white dressing gown. Allen hops over, holding his bleeding foot. Not *bleeeeeding*, actually *bleeding*.

'You're bleeding all over the place!'

I know, it's caused by your bleeding bust pot, he considers saying but doesn't.

'Don't get blood on the tiles,' orders Grace, 'you know where the bleeding bathroom is.'

Allen hobbles off to the bathroom trying not to goose step. The scorpion is in fact a scorpion, however it is by no means a monster of its breed contrary to Grace's previous forensics description. A wee beast a mere fifteen millimetres long, hardly a raptor of its species, and really quite an offence to kill if size does in fact matter after all. Still, Allen removes his non-bloody flip-flop and performs a quick Björn-Borg backhand on the poor creature. Prior to match point, Allen slips on Grace's shower gel "with a hint of jojoba and ginseng", obviously misplaced in her hasty retreat from the bathroom. Allen flails for the first available thing to ease the inevitable fall: the faux linen suspended curtain held up by an antique walnut-veneer ciel de lit which covered the shower end of the charming, scorpion-infested, roll top bath decorated with brass ball and claw feet. The ciel de lit, not known for its strength or use as a mountaineering aid, detaches from the ceiling and hits Allen on the head just above the right eye, which starts to bleed all over the white faux linen. He looks like some ng out of Ghost Busters. Thankfully, the vintage eighteenth centu ciel de lit remains intact, unlike Allen's bleeding head which now r ches his foot.

W e the fuck has the scorpion pissed off too, Allen frankly doesn ive a toss. *Probably in my Bermuda shorts*. To add insult not only t ermuda but his injury too, Grace, how very helpful, shouts in that d awful screech of hers.

'H you caught the bastard yet, you seem to be making a hell of a n in there!'

'Bi job than I thought!' Allen replies, trying to fix the shower canop e ciel de lit and his bleeding foot and eye. *Good job it ain't foot an uth.*

'To ou it was a big bastard!' Shouts Grace.

Tha what the ciel de lit thinks.

'Mr n, I'll soon be done, Mrs Houseman-Smith, do you have any pla ?

5
The Windy Bar

Allen's drive back to the bar is uncomfortable but thankfully uneventful. The poet Anthony is still in the same position: drinking, sitting in the shade at the same table, the one with the best panoramic view but furthest from the bar, which is empty. Anthony's gaze is lost in the sea. Allen observes a bowl of half-consumed black olives, a bowl of chips and a partially-eaten pack of Ginger Nuts. A strange dietary combination. Allen didn't think one could buy them here in Kea. Mateo strolls over.

'Christ, buddy, what you been doing?' He is genuinely concerned about the tour rep's general health, appearance, and recent scorpion battle. Make a great B movie, forgive the insect pun. Allen tells him about the scorpion tale, exaggerating as shamelessly as Grace.

Allen loves the Windy Bar, particularly at the end of the season, only a couple of months before everything winds down. Not that the island is particularly busy anyway. He checks his watch, he has a late arrival coming. A few late arrivals rather, one of which is a couple arriving together. Hopefully it is the Crawfords.

Margaritte and Denholm Crawford. They have both been to Kea many times before. Same place, same time of year, both getting more decrepit with each visit. They are a game old pair though, both retired watercolour painters who drink ready-mixed gin and tonic they carry in Schweppes' Tonic Water bottles wrapped in newspaper as some kind of primitive chiller for their painting days. They usually hire a car from the improbably-named Fantasy Car Rentals, which is always a modest knacker of a thing and certainly no vehicular fantasy. Their car is already at their villa, with the keys in the ignition rather than at reception. Denholm and Margaritte always insist on being picked up and escorted home, not back to Wiltshire but to the Villa Amaryllis. Allen knows their car will be fine unlocked and keyed up, who would nick it on Kea after all? And if they did, where would they go? A twenty-minute drive takes them around the island; certainly not the Tour De France.

Strangely, or call it coincidence considering poet Anthony's Ginger Nuts, but the Crawfords are big time cracker fanatics, the cheese cracker people of the world. They used to be in the business until Denholm sold the company. Not to mention, they are in fact crackers themselves, but in a lovely, eccentric, old English world sort of way; with a hint of Stilton.

6
Hebes and Penelope

Three missed calls, two texts and a partridge up your jacksie. Allen wakes up at five am, as usual, to attend to his business, his and no one else's.

'Only another four months to Christmas!' Allen recants aloud.

Internally, he is thinking about his favourite hotel in the heart of Metaxourgeio, Athens, the beating heart of the pinkish red-light district of the city. And the workplace of Penelope Barbas, his part-time girlfriend, as per an arrangement that seems to suit both her and Allen admirably. Yet they do like each other. Providing Lady Penelope doesn't bring the pink Rolls Royce, or Parker, for that matter. Allen is very fond of Penne, his cutesy name for her, although on occasions, and probably due to overt wine intoxication, he does mispronounce it as *Pele*, after the most brilliant Brazilian footballer. While Penne does favour a full Brazilian, she finds the mistake vaguely irritating.

The main problem with Metaxa, as Allen calls the place, is not its name or the brandy, which he is most comfortable with, excluding the blood pressure and the hangover, but the fact that one has to be reasonably circumspect in one's choice of partner. Allen discovered this first-hand after inviting Cora Evangeline Roma back to his hotel room at the four-point-four star-rated Acropolis Plaza Smart. Cora, in fact, turned out to have slightly more than Allen had bargained for, namely a healthy and very firm eight-inch penis clad in Oroblu Repos 70 control top support hosiery. The experience, although slightly confusing, had been interesting. Perhaps not to be repeated, but interesting nonetheless. The support pants being very necessary afterwards as the sweet Lady Boy had huge hairless balls.

Back to the calls then. Why does Grace, the absolute fucking lunatic want: A) the villa heated in the middle of August; B) require a complete, or so it seems, makeover of the kitchen area; and C) the crystal-clear pool to be chlorinated again, with some industrial toxic stuff that would ultimately bleach her already leather-red and partially-tanned skin back to white. Apparently, she wants the same stuff they use at home, which is probably neat acid and possibly why she is as white as a bichon frisé. *It's a miracle she has got any hair left at all.*

Dear Lord, Allen thinks whilst driving back to the Bougainvillea, *why won't this wretched woman just leave me the fuck alone!*

He deliberately spins the transit slightly to raise the dust below the terrace. He disembarks, slamming the door as loud as possible without detaching it and limps onto the patio. He admires Nikos's tidy handy job on the once historic pot whilst he considers acid baths, kitchen decoration and Grace's personal sanity.

'Alleeeeeen.' That oh-so-familiar grating squawk greets him from somewhere behind, or possibly below, a large white flowering hebe.

In Greek mythology, Hebe was one of Zeus's daughters, the Goddess of eternal youth. Allen wanders over to the once fine shrub that has now been desecrated by Grace's fat ass.

'I don't think the Goddess would have been pleased to discover your feet sticking out the top of her plant.'

'Got miself bleeding stuck looking for one of mi contacts!' Her eyes wander idly over Allen. 'This fucking euphoria ain't one of the poisonous ones, is it?'

'No it's not. It's a hebe.' Allen couldn't give a monkey's ass if it were poisonous. 'The other plant you're speaking of is actually called a euphorbia.' But he did wonder if euphorbias would in fact grow in Greece. There was one variety called the *Spiny Sponge* and this plant is, or rather was, definitely a hebe.

'I don't need a frigging nature lesson, Allen. Bleeding "Tit-Marsh". Just help me get out this fucker!'

Allen offers his firm hand to assist her removal. *How I wish the fucker would poison her.*

Allen receives the text from Penelope, his occasional yet lovely babe, while on the way back to the Windy Bar. He had advised Grace that the pool would be done which it won't, the heating can be turned on, which it can't, and the kitchen will be redecorated for her hopeful return next season, which it won't.

'Thinking of coming over for a few days, are you cool with that?' Allen

feels a tingle in his Rip Curl Mirage Cure, twenty-inch surfing shorts which are in fact a thirty-two inch waist and somewhat hard to come by. Luckily, he has managed to find some.

'Yeah Honey Girl, but I ain't paying.' Allen is not much of a romantic.

'It's all on me, Big Man.'

Allen certainly hopes this is the case. *'When are you coming, sweet pants?'*

'As soon as I get a feel for that strange cock of yours,' she replies.

Penny, although earning her income in a vaguely unorthodox way—and we are not talking the Greek Church here—, is in no way anyone's fool. She has a degree in ballet dancing from the Maria Pothitou School of Dance in Athens, which kind of helps with the pole dancing. It is all in the wrists apparently, not the breasts. Although she does own an abundance of breasts. Not Francisco Scaramanga 007 big though. Allen thinks of her doing a *pas de deux* without the tutu and the pointe shoes and feels the earth move. Well, not quite the earth but somewhere even closer to home.

'Get here fast, babe, I miss you. I miss you and I'm paying for everything apart from your cute butt, please bring those high black shoes.' He eagerly replies.

'Okay. Get nice and hard sex doll I'm riding that dolphin soon.'

7
Beach showers and the Devil

Allen needs to visit the beach shower, the only one on Kea which fortunately is just opposite the Windy Bar to cool things down in his shorts. Allen notices the poet watching and hopes he can't see his bulging shorts and the strange vibration in the back pocket. He turns on the water and feels the sun-heated water cool his brains as well as his erection. But there is still a buzzing occurring in his backside area, almost a ringing.

'Shit, shit, shit, buggery shit!' Allen shouts, desperately trying to turn the water off.

Now, as most people know, Greek plumbing is somewhat complex even though their culture, mythology, ancient history and war record are both outstanding and immense. All they need are a few pissing plumbers with a reasonable idea of how to do the plumbing and they would be laughing. No more rank-smelling bin next to the loo with soiled tissue and sanitary matter oozing out.

The shower tap refuses to turn off despite Allen's efforts. The fucker has gripped, and suddenly snaps off completely, sending a jet of pressurised cold water into Allen's already-sodden nut sack, permeating further into his mobile phone pocket. Temporarily forgotten but now remembered and housed in his shorts back pocket. It's from Grace how-fucking-ridiculously-timed Houseman-Smith. Her contact details on the display with the subtext Allen added earlier, *the Devil*.

The things that still work: his erection, his phone. The things that don't: the beach shower and Grace how's-your-bleeding-Father Smith meeting the mighty Kenneth Williams. Allen's phone is a Nokia, chrome case with autoflip access. It is incredibly cool, unlike Allen, and apparently waterproof, unlike Allen.

'You, fucking bute!' Allen screams, clutching the phone to his lips like it was Penelope or even the huge-breasted Saffron. *Careful*, thinks Allen as he imagines an epic adventure with both these beautiful nymphs together. *Wake up you old fool, put it out of your mind ... not the phone! The other thing! You're just too sodding old for that type of caper. Fix the fucking tap.*

The recorded message from Grace not only shrieks his name but adds even more "*e*" to it than usual. Not talking about substance abuse here.

'Is the tour guide excursion meeting still on at the Windy Bar tomorrow at ten? Cos I'm bored.'

Shit I forgot about that, the bitch can obviously read. Allen imagines Grace underlining various sections of the Welcome Hospitality Brochure, in fluorescent yellow, to match her snakeskin eyes.

'Alleeeeen! I would like you to organise some trips!'

Allen thinks: A) the Titanic, B) the Marie Celeste, C) a desert island or D), the fucking Moon.

'I wanna consult the Oracle of Delphi,' Grace orders.

Part of Allen is quite impressed by her grasp of history, another part of him thinks that Delphi is fucking miles from Kea, in upper-central Greece on a plateau along the slope of Mount Parnassus. It is also the sanctuary of Apollo, the God of light, knowledge and harmony; everything Grace does not have. Although she does need housing in a NASA rocket and sending to Mars. Another Allen does wonder why Grace needs the Oracle when she persistently badgers him all the time. Allen rings her.

'Be there at nine thirty,' Mrs Houseman-History-Smith orders.

'The other guests will be attending,' comments Allen, hoping this will shut her up.

'Fuck the others.' She abruptly ends the call.

Feeling slightly nauseous, Allen contacts the Crawfords, the glorious Saffron and the muscle-bound Kevin, poet Anthony and Bret, the disillusioned landscape gardener from the very south of Derbyshire who finally turned up, only two days late and incidentally all his fault. He had looked like he had been in a serious fight with a fig tree or some large plant of that kind.

'Gardening truly sucks,' Bret said.

'Right on squire,' replied Allen knowing the form.

'Slab the sodding lot, cover it with cement, tarmac, crazy fucking paving, I don't give a shite. "Save the planet" my arse. I'm sure it can save itself without my topiary skills and five tree-planting techniques.' He moaned.

'Bollocks! Just don't deck the fucker.'

'In England it'll last two years tops before the rain rots it to buggery.' Not only was Bret a talented, yet unenthusiastic gardener, but he was also a qualified first aider and had played rugby football for a couple of seasons for the Crofters in Burton-on-Trent, the latter two testimonials walking hand-in-hand. To Bret, his present injuries were nothing unusual, almost trivial.

'I picked these cuts and bruises up in Lavrion, that's why I'm a bit late. I think I was unconscious for a day, but I can't really remember.' Bret had stared off into space trying to recollect his forgotten memories, before quickly giving up and shaking his head. 'Anyway, it's nice to be on Kea finally. Thanks for picking me up.'

8
Lunch and "Journey"

Allen decides the best possible plan is to eat lunch at the Windy Bar. Mateo won't mind that he is drenched, and the wind will hopefully dry him out. Anthony eyes him vaguely and suspiciously as he wonders over to the pool-side bar, leaving a trail of water behind him.

'You've busted the beach shower tap again, haven't you Allen?' Mateo eyes Allen's sodden shorts, the wet Nokia phone, and the red beach tap in his left hand.

'Sorry Mateo, I'll get Nikos to sort it. I've wedged the hole where the tap has sheared off with a bit of wood. I've stuck it into the pipe.'

'What is sheared? Isn't it something you do with goats or sheep?'

'Well, yes, but not quite in this instance,' Allen replies. 'It has two meanings, in this case nothing to do with animals.'

'Oh…' Responds Mateo.

Allen wonders if he should continue with the complete explanation but thinks maybe the conversation regarding the hair-trimming may end up being more complex and conclude with a talk about Brazilian's. He then thinks of Penelope, his antique pine kitchen table, a pack of yellow Bic razors and the busted beach-side shower. Almost a Buddhist's complete life circle. Instead of giving further English lessons, he orders tzatziki, Greek fries, and a cheeseburger.

'Preferably not one of your goats, Mateo,' Allen clearly adds. 'And a big Mythos, please.'

Mateo raises an eyebrow and duly obliges with the beer before disappearing behind the chain curtain at the back of the bar separating the room from the kitchen and the goats. Allen's phone rings again, with a slight new gurgle to its tone. The display reads "The Devil".

'Jesus fucking Christ!' Allen rather inappropriately shouts in sheer disbelief at Grace's harassing behaviour. *Aren't there laws for this?*

He turns his phone off whilst Mateo slaughters the goat and Allen fantasises sacrificing Grace on the ancient black altar he had discovered on one of his archaeological adventures.

It was truly an amazing place in a disused and deserted chapel that had somehow collapsed partially off the cliff edge and then submerged itself into the ground. Allen had dangerously gained access by hauling himself off the cliff and into the gaping mouth of Greek history and Christian faith, always a hungry beast to feed. The altar was truly beautiful, black marble supported left and right by ancient Doric columns, mythology adapted to Christianity, like a sort of religious recycling, or like ancient Druidic places in the UK, a Norman church banged on top of an ancient burial mound but with the great ancestors, the sons and daughters of the Wicca, the offspring of the craft, the fine and first planted yew, the tree of death. The chapel he discovered still possessed the twelfth century frescos on the remaining part of the vaulted ceiling, open to the elements, the sea, wind, all except people, which was a real shame.

Mateo brings over the tzatziki, bread, some napkins, and a paper tablecloth which he fixes to the table with special chrome clips.

'The burger and fries will arrive shortly.' He grandly announces. 'Do you want some fried zucchini?'

'Why not,' says Allen. The Mythos is iced cold and tastes great.

With a rather soggy, half-eaten burger, Anthony wheels himself over in an uneasy and wobbly fashion. 'Can't get done in Greece driving these things, even with faulty brakes. Mind if I join you? I've had a few! Just love Ouzo, could drink it til the cows come home and carry on after they have been milked. Who really needs milk anyway? I wrote a poem. Want to hear it?'

Allen knows he has no choice, he is a captive audience and, unlike Grace's phone harassment, he can't turn him off unless he suffocates the poet with the remaining part of his soggy burger. A happy meal indeed.

'Take it away Anthony,' Allen says noticing Mateo, obviously a fan, wandering over to listen.

'It's called "Journey" which, Allen, for you being a tour rep is really quite up your street, no pun intended.'

Journey

Picture eternity,

so still but for a whispered bitter cry,
we fall screaming,
through a vision in blue of all sea and sky.
To clutch at a thousand easy moments,
on the road that leads always—

Anthony splutters and Allen interrupts, 'Get him another Ouzo, Mateo, for Christ's sake, this is rather fine!'

Anthony raises his empty glass to Allen. 'Sorry old boy,' he splutters again, 'and thanks Mateo, you beautiful man.'

Mateo duly returns with a triple measure and a separate bowl of ice.

'Where did we get to then,' asks the poet, taking a large gulp of Ouzo and ignoring the ice.

'On the road that leads always...' replies Allen.

'Ah yes, that eternal road!' Replies the poet.

...
on the road that leads all ways,
in this place,
our tiny ship of time.

Together again then,
with the woman in shadow who patiently waits.
She no less like a rose of delicate beauty,
turns to leave,
weeping love, aching from a summers rain.
I remember now she told me once—

Mateo coughs. 'Very sorry,' he says. Allen's muted phone starts to vibrate loudly again. He ignores it and spreads his hands towards the poet in a gesture of apology, inviting him to proceed. Anthony continues, unfazed.

...
trip out here my dearest friend.

Your life is nothing but the dark forest,
and although the wind is sometimes sad, [Anthony growls]
as cold as the moon,
in our together garden,
we will forever sing after the light.

For as long as the journey takes.

Allen thinks about Delphi, the Oracle, the journey, and Grace, vibrating in his now dry shorts. There is a long and poignant pause, the proverbial dropping pin could have been heard.

'Well,' asks Anthony, 'do I get this one on the house or not?' Raising his depleted Ouzo to the light.

'On the house certainly!' Congratulates Mateo.

'That was truly beautiful! You're not Greek by any chance, are you?' Allen adds, actually thinking that it was bloody good.

'Benefits of a quality education, old boy,' says Anthony. 'No! No three "R"s there. Can say the same about the three "B"s: bullying, bigotry and buggery. But at least we had a squash court and no dear Mateo. Unfortunately I'm not Greek, but I will have another large Ouzo!

'What is squash?' Mateo asks.

Here we go again… Allen looks at his phone, wondering whether to answer Grace's vibrating or if he even dares to.

'A pointless game with small black rubber balls, four walls and a couple of rackets.' Anthony says.

Glad I don't have to explain! Thinks Allen as he remembers the interesting night with Cora Evangeline Roma in Athens.

'Sorry people, I have to turn this thing back on from mute, count to ten, then answer Houseman!' He silently gets to nine before the bastard rings again. She really was the Devil.

'Alleeeeeeeen! Is there a chemist on this God forsaken bleedin' island? We've both got thrush!'

Allen retches, feeling Mateo's unhappy burger moving back up. Anthony leans across the table and grabs his arm.

'You okay, old man?

'Mm,' replies Allen, reaching for a block of ice from the poet's bowl, and turns the phone off. 'Indigestion,' he lies. 'Should have taken some Rennies.'

'I can order you one of those!' Offers Anthony. 'A damn fine idea actually! Two Remies, Mateo!' He shouts at the vibrating chain curtain separating the bar, the kitchen, and the goats.

Thrush. An innocent, sweet, enchanting name for such an unfortunate condition. A songbird with discharge. Mateo returns with another Ouzo, the brandy and an apology.

'Sorry, only Metaxa, no Remy.'

Allen thinks of Cora again and the pink light district of Athens.

'Thanks Mateo, but I really shouldn't, I'm on duty.'

'You're not a sodding police officer, old boy!' Anthony pipes up. 'Drink it, you look like you need it. Now, I'll leave you to your call on that bloody wretched thing. I swear, too much communication will ultimately cause the world to expire.'

Allen looks at the drink, then at his phone. He slugs back the brandy in one shot.

'Rat down a drain! Good man!' Shouts Anthony over his shoulder as he wobbles away, busted brakes and all, no doubt to compose another journey on another planet.

9
THRUSH

Allen presses re-dial. It only rings twice. *The bitch must have the fucker strapped to her head!*

'You took your bleedin' time Alleeeeen!'

'Sorry, bad signal.' He lies.

'Is there a friggin chemist here or what, you tool!'

Really, tool? 'Well yes, but it's closed today. Have you tried Greek yoghurt for your mutual condition?'

'What, to fucking eat? Course I av!'

'No,' says Allen patiently, 'apply it directly to the inflamed area.'

'What, with honey?'

'No! Just plain old yoghurt, no chives, no garlic, nothing. Just pure yoghurt. And make sure it's not old or out of its sell-by date.'

'Yeah, done that.' She says. 'It's pink ain't it?'

Give me strength...

'No, it's white. What you've used is taramasalata, which is salted cod roe, not a good idea at all.'

'Crap! I've just wedged Christian's knob in a pot of the stuff. Dirty bastard, that's who I've got it from. He's outside now, looking like an oversized bagel with his stuff hanging out, pretending to read The Guardian. It's upside down, not his balls or his thing but the out-of-date newspaper.'

Allen hears a loud thudding noise and a shatter of glass in the background, followed by Grace's voice in maximum falsetto screeching. 'Christian, what the fuck have you done now?'

Jesus, what next? Allen hears Christian mumbling something about Greek yoghurt and his hip. Grace manages to come back to the phone.

'Hang on Allen, go nowhere and shut up.' Allen goes nowhere and "shuts up". Grace is back within thirty seconds. 'The daft bastard. The complete twat! He's only gone and slipped on Greek yoghurt and hurt his friggin leg!'

'Don't you mean taramasalata?' Allen politely enquires. 'You could try Canesten?'

'A can of what?'

'No, *Canesten*!' His patience is wearing thin.

'Afghanistan, for his leg, bit far to go innit!'

'No! *Canesten*! For the infection, but the pharmacy is closed today.'

'You're breaking up!' Squawks Grace.

Sounds more like you are. 'Try the pharmacy tomorrow. It's next to the cash machine in the harbour, just down from the Windy Bar.'

10
TOUR MEETING AND CHIPS

'Greetings, dear people!' Allen looks around the group, feeling nervous. Public speaking is not his forte. 'Has anyone seen Bret? The injured and most elusive gardener from Derbyshire?'

Anthony the poet, Saffron the Goddess, muscle-bound Kevin, who is busy flexing, the crazy Crawfords, engrossed in their paintings, and of course the very, very charming red Grace Houseman, currently without her husband Christian, who has supposedly put his hip out, shake their heads. No one knows where Bret is, although the Crawfords say they recall seeing him bathing naked not so long ago during their morning landscape painting adventures. Mateo pours out complimentary piña coladas. He has had to use goat's milk as stocks of coconut milk were unfortunately running low. He hopes no one would notice. Christian enters, smoking a cigar.

'Sorry everyone. A bit late, I know. Just been to the pharmacy, the wife's got thrush.' Allen looks at Grace, surprised she has not yet reacted to Christian's overly informative excuse. Instead, she looks unaffected as he limps over and sits on the faded rattan chair next to her.

Mateo disappears behind the chain curtain with a puzzled expression, probably trying to figure out what thrush was. He returns rather quickly, his confusion disappeared, carrying a large tray containing bowls of Greek fries, black olives, fried zucchini and some dolmades, which everyone apart from Allen ignores. Christian relights his large cigar and Allen raises his glass to his guests.

'*Yamas*!'

Allen can't help but notice that Christian keeps patting his crotch like Michael Jackson but without the glove and certainly not moon-walking.

'Welcome good people, may all your dreams be fulfilled on our truly beautiful island of Kea!'

'Al'wight get on wiv it, Allen!' Expresses Grace, knocking back the first piña colada in a matter of five seconds. Mateo refills her glass, and she looks relieved. 'Cum on, Allen.' She looks at his attire and smirks. 'That Hawaiian shirt looks well boss on you.'

Allen ignores her. The shirt had been bought in Athens, a present from Penelope, who Allen is meeting on the ferry later, along with two other guests, Finisterre and Alistair Thompson, aka the Thompson Twins. Allen hopes they don't bring sodding Tintin.

He briefly runs through the safety rules which have already been ignored in full by all of Allen's audience. He receives some simple polite Greek responses and helps them correct their pronunciation and educate them on the meaning of some friendlier words. These, however, are immediately translated from his Greek to Grace's Essex tongue. For instance, the Greek for "thank you" is "*efharisto*". For Grace, it is "effing Harry's toe", just like "*parakalo*" becomes "parrots are low". The best of Grace's Greek is "Gazzer's Gizmo". Mercifully, everyone seems to know Gazza and how to ask for the bill in Greece, "*logariasmios*". Allen finally gets to the itinerary of the tour. There is only one: the Kea Boat Tour.

'The Kea Boat Tour involves a beautiful beach stop at the deserted Vroskopos Beach for swimming, drinks and a barbecue. Then on to Karthea, an ancient city ruin that still functioned up until the Byzantine period. At one point, Karthea was a walled city with six entrances all guarded by huge towers to protect it from invasion. It was one of the most important cities in Ancient Greece and home to a Doric temple dedicated to the goddess Saffron, sorry,' Allen coughs, forgetting his script. 'I mean, the goddess Athena, in the sixth century BCE and the Pythian Temple of Apollo, five hundred and thirty BCE.'

Grace yawns, the poet looks fascinated, Kevin is still flexing, *clearly more testosterone than brain*, Christian flicks cigar ash into what is left of the chips, the Crawfords are taking a nap in their matching beanie hats and Saffron proceeds to file her nails with a nail block. So Allen continues with more enthusiasm.

'It even has its own ruined amphitheatre that dates back to the first century...'

He purposefully coughs and the Crawfords wake up with a start and say, 'We're in, we'll paint!'

Anthony intervenes. 'Can they get me and the chair in old boy, without being a pain in the ass? And more importantly get me off the bugger and up to the ruins?'

Allen laughs. 'I'm sure you'll be fine, buddy, I'll carry you if needs be.'

'You're a fine fellow. Mateo, dear chap, get us another Ouzo, will you! I can't drink anymore of this goat milk stuff'

'Oh, I fancy the beach and some off-boat diving, can we do that too?' Saffron enquires. Allen gets slightly hot under the collar, Kevin just grunts and flexes a bicep, Christian continues to stroke his crotch in a most unpleasant fashion and Grace says in a rather spoiled child sort of way, 'But I want to go to Delphi to consult the Oracle about mi future, Alleeeen, aw wight!'

'It's a long, long way from here, sorry Mrs Houseman-Smith.'

'Look, just shut up and make it happen. Christian is friggin' loaded, hire a boat or sum'at, jus' do it, will ya.'

Allen holds up his hands to calm the tantrum. 'Okay, okay,' he adds in sheer desperation as Grace's empty glass looks somewhat poised for chucking. 'I'll talk to Yannis, he's the man with the boats, and see if we can sort it for you.'

'I really need to consult the Oracle,' Grace repeats.

The only consultant you need to consult is a good psychiatrist, Allen thinks.

'I've got a poem about that!' Adds Anthony helpfully.

Allen looks at the aging, thinning, grey-haired, bespectacled poet with warmth and inwardly thanks him for his input and distraction but decides now is not the time for a poetry reading. 'Not now Anthony, maybe later.'

The Meltemi blows again, wafting that sweet Cypress tree and wild fennel-enthused air, with the salty scent of the Aegean over, and under, the white sail awning of the Windy Bar. Allen's guests with the exception of the tree-hating Bret from South Derbyshire, who will probably be waiting on the beach, naked, to greet Allen's entourage, all sign up for the Kea Boat Tour. They all depart back to their holidays apart from Anthony, who wheels his way to the bar with a multi-pack of black ballpoint pens and a Tesco's A4 notepad. Allen watches as Kevin fires up his recently-hired Honda NX650 Dominator with cradle frame, swing arm and seating for two. *Bastard. He must have a small cock.* The glorious Saffron languidly slips onto the throbbing machine to clutch at Kevin's broad, tanned shoulders. No helmet, no care, no worries, just off for some more private naked bathing. The thought slightly bitters Allen.

He observes the piña colada-fuelled Grace stagger to the pharmacy and smoking Christian read a newspaper upside down by the harbour wall. He mentally motivates himself. Penne is coming later; "coming" being the operative word. That is, after he has ditched the Thompson Twins.

11
Yannis, Penelope and the Thompsons

'I realise it's a fuck of a way to go, but can you do it for the spoilt cow? Her husband is loaded.'

'What is loaded?' Enquires Yannis whilst trying to beat a rather large piece of metal flat with an equally large lump hammer.

'Okay,' says Allen, 'imagine a gun ready to fire but stuffed with money instead of bullets.'

'Calm down, my friend, calm down.' Yannis holds out his arms in a gesture of appeasement. 'This is Kea, not Kegwort Derbys Shure.'

'Has Bret been in?' Allen thinks the Derbyshire reference is too much of a coincidence.

'I know no one called Bread,' confirms Yannis.

'Okay.' *Maybe not.* 'Anyway, this is a private charter. It could be very lucrative, we could both make some serious money here, you could add a twenty percent finder's fee for me.'

Yannis, tall, strong, very bearded, very Greek, somewhere between Jethro Tull and ZZ Top with a fine George Clooney moustache and one very large gold tooth, strokes his beard. 'What is "lucrative"?'

Jesus Christ, 'Big dollars.'

'Ah I see,' replies Yannis, 'big folding cash. No problem then, leave it with me and ten percent.'

'No, twenty percent.'

Yannis strokes his beard. 'Okay,' he agrees. 'It will take at least four to five hours at sea and then a taxi charter.'

'Fuck,' answers Allen thinking of Penelope. 'I ain't going then.'

'You don't have to, leave it to me, man. We need the big boat though, the white one, it's not cheap.'

'Is it fixed? I thought it had some problem with the fuel line and the bow had a slight dent in it.'

'No, absolutely fine now, Allen! Don't worry mate, all fixed.'

Allen organised the Kea beach and ancient ruin trip on a small boat called the Zephyr, the god of the west wind. He felt reasonably upbeat, so he arranged the oracle trip on the Boreas, a big white boat named after another wind god, the god of the north wind, which is quite apt to carry the oh-so-boring Houseman-Smiths.

Allen discreetly whiffs his under arm. 'Mmm,' he concludes aloud. He needs a shower, and maybe a new personality—that one is actually a definite—, some new clothes, money, and a fucking clean home … *Shit!* Penne will be here in a couple of hours and he still had to change the linen on his crusty bed and wash all the friggin' stuff in the sink. He looked at his reflection in Yannis' dusty window at his receding elegance with a hint of intelligence. No need for a haircut.

Back to the bakery, the wonderful aroma of the morning's freshly baked bread still lingers in the air, as does something stale and decidedly unpleasant. It greets Allen as he opens the front door. His silent Yamaha DX7 welcomes him in the narrow hall that leads to the kitchen and lounge area. It is not quite a piano but he can play it well.

'Shit, that fucking fish!' Allen remembers. 'Where've I put the bastard!' He recalls buying it two days ago before Grace arrived. Even Allen had to chuckle when he found the fish on top of the fridge, not inside.

With the fish out, bedding changed, a bottle of Dolce & Gabbana Bi sprayed everywhere and some Bougainvillea in an old jug on the antique pine table, Allen is satisfied with his quick clean. He checks the bathroom a final time, which evokes him the memory of Penne's last visit. He locates his Bic's razors. The toilet is pristine, the shit basket next to toilet is empty with clean bag. Penelope is a lady. He puts the toilet seat down.

12
THE HARBOUR IN KORISSIA AT NIGHT

The lights in the harbour, from the taverna's fairy lamps and candles, tickle and blaze their shimmer across the black water of the slowly rippling bay of St. Nikolaos. On his way past the tobacco and newspaper kiosk, Allen notices that Yannis has moored the big boat. The beautiful white lugger with the mahogany internal veneer. The one called the Boreas is docked in deep water to accommodate the sleek keel of the craft. It is tied to the inverted cannon from a previous battle, with submerged embrasures set deep within the concrete. It now serves as mooring ties and parking bollards on the promontory that juts out into the black sea.

Allen observes the activity around the craft. There is a local engineering van with a faded, painted sign of the company's name, *No Problem Marines Engineering*, accommodating labourers working a late shift on the Boreas. There was plenty of time before the trip. Thinking about time, Allen remembers a line from one of Anthony's poems. *"Time is all we have, time to live, time to die, time to fly with Avion Bleu."* Allen is not quite sure what it means, but for some reason it has stuck in his mind.

The Flying Dolphin, hopefully containing his dear Penne and the Thompson Twins, is on time from Lavrion. He watches as the mighty beast drops down from its hydrofoil skies and calmly enters the harbour to dock past the Boreas. The alarm of the harbour rings to indicate its arrival, an alert not louder than the average Leicester City football air horn.

Allen makes his way to the designated spot with his tatty Laskarina Holidays sign to waive at the Thompsons, hoping that dear Penelope will still recognise him without it. It has been a while since she has seen his face. The cabin crew lowers the boarding ramps for the chaos of off-boarding and on-boarding to start. Allen's phone rings with its usual foul timing. It is the equally foul Grace. The Devil. Allen answers.

'Wot's the point of 'aving a phone if you never answer the fucker?' As usual, she answers with her standard polite greeting.

'Sorry, but I'm down at the harbour to pick up some new guests.'

'So what? Answer your bastard phone! That's why it's called a mobile, so you can answer it while you're mobile.' Allen considers this, as well as asking how the thrush is going, but then decides against it.

'What can I do for you, Mrs Houseman-Smith?'

'Welllll Alleeeeeen, me and Chris, meaning Christian, are going to the fucking church at Pangy Katri tomorrow.'

Oh crap. 'Do you mean the Monastery of Panagia Kastriani? That's about twelve kilometres from Kea's capital on the north side of the island, you'll need a car.'

'Got a jeep, it's white like mi sandals. Where is it this Monastery thing?'

'It's clearly marked on the map that's in your welcome pack. It's easy enough to find and vaguely signposted in a Greek sort of way but the roads are unsurfaced, so take it slow.'

Allen sees what undeniably has to be the Thompson Twins hauling various silver suitcases off the craft and an even larger and heavy-looking one that has required the assistance of an annoyed boarding official. They lug it down the gangway from boat to dry land.

'Sorry Mrs Houseman, my guests have arrived so I have to go.' He turns the phone off with sympathetic thoughts for the resident priest who oversees the Monastery, the monks and nuns having vacated years before.

In his mind, Allen had already visualised the Thompson Twins. He was somewhat surprised when they appeared looking nothing like his preconceptions of two René Magritte, bowler hatted surrealists. They were clearly twins though, both handsome, both dark-haired with close-cropped military-style haircuts, loose-fitting combat fatigues in black and Hells Angels t-shirts. The tops were not identical but similar. Both were well-worn but clean. They wore low Dr. Martens without socks. In Allen's mind, no socks was equivalent to tough. From what Allen could tell, they were both pretty handy in the muscle department. He wickedly considers introducing the pair to Kevin. He notices they both carry large, hard-shelled cases and wonders what might be inside. He holds out his hand to greet Finisterre Thompson.

'Call me Finn. And this is Alistair, call him Alise, with an "S", this is important,' he adds with menace in his voice. 'His temperament is not as chilled as mine.'

Alistair shakes Allen's hand, who buckles slightly under the pressure.

'Good to meet you, gents. I'm Allen. What's with all the gear?'

'Our business,' says Finn, noticing a vaguely untraceable accent.

Allen, clearly not getting the message, continues blissfully undaunted. 'And what business is that?'

The Thompson Twins look at each other with tired eyes and retort in perfect unison, 'The oil business.'

'What, like BP, Shell, ExxonMobil?' Allen is still off-message.

'No, olive oil.' Alise growls like a pit bull. How apt, the Thompsons and olive oil. Allen finally receives the "keep out" vibe.

'Allen!' A voice of beauty rises above the brief bustle of the port. 'Sex doll, where are you?' The voice sounds like home, it could be love but it certainly is his occasional but only true babe, Penelope.

'Ah that will be me!' Allen confirms to Finn and Alise, who look at him with new-found admiration as the most elegant Penne approaches with attitude. She looks well hot. *And we ain't talking perspiration here,* although Allen is sweating.

'Great babe,' says Alise. Is she taken?'

'All mine!' Confirms Allen. 'You stick with your cases whilst I greet her.

Allen heaves his way through the crowd of people going on and off the ferry. He knows what's coming off later, that pristine tight white blouse and those black Capri Pants.

Penelope Barbas looks like the stunt double for Uma Thurman. Olive skin, deep, mysterious brown eyes, sleek jet black hair cut in a shoulder-length sixties bob, scarlet red lipstick on oh-so-kissable lips and high black heels. As requested, she even smokes! Mainly Gauloises. Allen embraces her. He inhales in her Diorissimo perfume, the vague trace of French cigarettes and something minty. He holds her close, and they kiss with passion. Finn coughs and Allen's phone starts to ring again. The Devil.

'Oh just fuck off,' mumbles Allen, breaking the embrace to check his phone. Penne looks surprised.

'What did you say?'

Allen, quick on the uptake, hastily answers. 'Sorry, not you peach.'

'We done here?' Alise enquires.

'Yeah, we're done. Let's wait for the commotion to calm a bit and I'll drive the van up here to collect you all, then drop you at your accommodation. But first, I must attend to Penne.'

Allen drops off Penne at the bakery. 'The flat is open and there's a bottle or six in the fridge. Use the Bollinger. You will find ice in the freezer, and you know where the champagne bucket is. Be a doll and light a few candles and fill the bath with bubbles.' Allen eyes her seductively. 'I'll be back after dropping them guys off.'

Alise and Finn get the benefit of a lovely cleavage shot as Penne leans through Allen's driver's side window and kisses him. 'Hurry back, *mon cher*.' She whispers. The twins look impressed as Penelope dexterously mounts the stairs adjacent to the bakery in high heels to gain access to Allen's flat which, as usual, is unlocked.

'Nice.' Finn is clearly impressed. 'Where'd you meet her?'

'Athens. Stop gawking.'

'Chill man, she's not my type! Beautiful yes, but not male enough for me.'

'Sorry fellas, I get kind of protective.'

'How far is it to the villa?' Asks Alise, tactfully changing the subject.

'Not far at all. Truthfully, nothing is really far on Kea. It's just finding what you're looking for that's the problem.'

'You a philosopher as well as a tour rep.' Grunts Finn.

'No bud, there are a few signposts on the island. Most are turned to lead the wrong way and that, my friend, is philosophy and life.' Allen waits but the twins show no sign of replying. 'Anyway, your villa is another ten-minute drive down this dirt track. It's pretty isolated.'

'Nothing wrong with isolation, unless of course you're not trying to escape a global pandemic,' says Finn. He points at his folded map of the island. 'The villa, it is on the beach here, isn't it?' Allen quickly looks at where Finn is pointing.

'Yep, that's the Villa Bergamot, famous for its orange and lemon trees. The boat you hired is already moored to the villa's private jetty.'

'Is it fuelled up?'

'The tank is full, I believe, but check first. You guys look like you know how to handle it.'

'Former Marines,' confirms Finn. Allen thinks about the cases, the Commandos, the muscle, Finn's sexuality and thinks best to shut the fuck up.

They arrive at the villa without incident. Finn and Alise decline the guided tour and seem more interested in stashing their gear. Allen fantasises about Penne waiting when the phone rings. It's the Devil again.

'You all cool then guys? I got to take this. There are some limited supplies inside; a couple of bottles, but you'll need a rig to get you into town to stock up unless you use the boat. There are some cards on the hall table with hire options.

'Thanks man,' says Finn. 'Leave us to it.'

Allen wonders what *it* is.

13
Power cuts and Penne

'The fucking power's off so we are in the pissing dark, Christian's shitfaced on some local home brew and I don't know what to do! I'm fucking hating all this! I was only trying to iron my bikini then everything went tits up!'

Allen looks at the lights in the other villas he passes, he looks at the harbour in the distance, its lights shimmering across the bay. *Who, on God's Earth, irons a sodding bikini?*

'I think I've grilled an iron wedgie in the fucker it was all pink and fluffy, now it's just, sort of melted brown.'

Christ. Allen runs his hand over his face. 'Please, Mrs Houseman, calm down. Turn the iron off and unplug it from the socket. Put it in the upright position and feel your way to the first overhead kitchen cabinet on the right. The one above the icon of Saint Teresa.'

'Who's Saint Gezza?'

'No, Teresa!' Allen shouts. 'I believe she was born Teresa Sánchez de Cepeda y Ahumada. She was Spanish.'

'Look, this is all very fucking interesting but I've got no bleedin lights!'

'Right, find the cabinet. There are candles, safety matches and a torch in there. Get the torch, walk to the hall, find the fuse box, it's on the right hand side of the front door, lift the lid and press whichever switch is down back up. It will be the only one that is facing the wrong way.' Allen hears stumbling, more glass broken.

'I've found the fucker.'

'Right, now locate that switch, say three Hail Mary, then turn the power back on.'

'It's on!' Squeals Grace with delight. Doltishly, she even said the Hail Mary. 'Aw thanks Alleeeen, you the man!'

'No problem. Now clear up the glass and, please, be careful. Good night … Oh! And don't use the iron again, I'll bring you a new one tomorrow.'

It's about nine-thirty in the evening by the time Allen gets back to the apartment. He eagerly confronts the stairs leading up to the flat, taking them two at a time. He is heavily panting by the time he reaches the door, God knows what his blood pressure is up to. The door is open, and Allen is greeted by a glorious aroma of fine cooking. Penne, looking truly beautiful in one of the Laskarina's white robes Allen had previously stolen, is sipping chilled champagne on the tiny balcony. Somewhat hanging uncomfortably—judging by the rust—over the bakery below, it is big enough to accommodate two recliners, a small potted lemon tree that Allen calls Russell, and a micro table, all accessible from the lounge by the louvred doors. Penne greets him warmly.

'It's only pasta, Sex Doll, but I'm sure you'll like it.'

'Well, you are Penne, princess of pasta, and my babe.' They embrace next to Russell. 'Christ, that feels good, hon. I was going to take you out for dinner but judging by the great smell in here, it looks like you've got it covered!'

Allen eyes Penne's robe seductively, touching the soft fabric thinly covering her breasts. 'I would, however, love to know what you've got covered under here.' Allen makes a pass to grab the robe's belt. He notices some sheer black stockings are protruding below the gown. Penne is too fast for him.

'You'll have to be a patient boy,' she says playfully. Her quick movements make the robe slide off her shoulder, and he notices she is wearing Agent Provocateur.

'Now, big man, do you want sex first or food?'

'Let's just skip the starter and main and go full-on to dessert!' Allen says, grabbing Penne and guiding her to the bedroom.

'Wait! Turn off the hob!'

'No need, babe. One is off and the other is on the boil. And I'm not talking pasta here!'

She giggles, the sound like a thousand wind chimes in a gentle breeze. Her orgasm makes Russell the lemon tree blush. Perhaps it was an orange tree after all.

Allen is in post-coital bliss, considering between pasta or round two. Penne looks spectacular in the Agent Provocateur, although Allen, in his enthusiasm, has put a good ladder in her left stocking. She doesn't know yet because it is on her back thigh, from his back shot action, a collateral damage. He feels the surge of the urge again just thinking about it. Before he can act on it, the Nokia, on the bed side table next to the fake Art Nouveau lamp, kicks in. It is sodding Grace again. She has left a voicemail. 'Alleeeen, where's the nearest petrol station cos we're doing this fucking monastery tomorrow.'

'Will you just stop harassing me, you wretched woman?'

'What?' Penne gasps, looking clearly hurt.

'Not you, peach! It's this god awful client, she just won't leave me alone.'

'What is her name? Do you want me to throat punch her?' She stands up and walks to the bathroom.

'Grace, and no, dearest, that won't be necessary.' He texts the Devil the direction to the nearest garage instead of calling her. He half-heartedly hopes she doesn't skank off with the altar candles or a few small icons of some long-dead saint.

'You've ripped my new stockings!' Penne shouts from the bathroom. 'Oh my stockings…' Her tone seems more humorous than before.

Allen smirks. 'It's still a good look though, babe. I'll buy you new ones, just don't take them off. And sorry, that phone thing is from the most irritating client I have ever known in all my time as Tour Rep Extraordinaire.'

She laughs. 'Well, you've certainly done an extraordinary Tour Rip of my stockings, you perv!'

Allen eventually decides to ring Grace and explain, very thoroughly, where the garage is, before hanging up before she has time to reply to his 'Gotta go, I'm getting a well needed service myself.'

They eat their pasta naked with a bottle of local red. Afterwards, he gives Penne oral on the lounge sofa and they make love a couple more times in the old Greek bed made in Coalbrookdale in the UK. They both fall asleep, half in half out of the old iron bed. The pots remain in the sink and Penne snuggles next to him still wearing her laddered stockings. Allen contently sighs, not wanting the night to end.

Penne wakes to the smell of coffee, fried bacon, burnt bread and

Allen playing something classical on the DX7. She grabs a robe and wanders to the kitchen, to find it tidy with the table laid.

'You're burning the bacon.' She says as she walks over to the cooker. 'And this sounds beautiful, by the way.'

'It's one of mine,' admits Allen. 'You actually like it?'

'Yes, it's fab, hon. We should get you sold to the highest publishing bidder, even if it's just for scientific research.'

14
Panagia Kastriani

The Monastery of Panagia Kastriani is located on the north side of Kea, about twelve kilometers from Ioulis, Kea's capital. This holy shrine of worship was built on the site of an old castle, hence the 'Kastri' part of the name, the Greek for 'castle'. According to local tradition, in around 1700, some shepherds had seen a light on top of the hill and climbed up to investigate, only to discover a source of light radiating from a specific point in the stony ground. They decided to dig it out. However after being well into the digging groove, they found an icon of the Virgin Mary and a can of Carlsberg—an untrue lager joke. In due course, a small church was built on the very spot, and it still remains today. A larger—not lager—church was built in 1912, with accommodations for its monks. Whilst Panagia Kastriani remains an operative place of worship, there are no longer any monks in residence, all having departed over the past forty years. Just one elderly Greek Orthodox priest remained, Father Basil Zenon. That's discounting the buried holy folks up there, of course. Basil in Greek means 'kingly', but Zenon has nothing to do with illumination or light fittings in this instance. The views are quite spectacular and the monastery itself is an oasis of peace and tranquillity. Until, of course, the How-How-Badly-Behaved-Housemans arrived on foot, both sweaty and very lightly clothed.

Father Basil Zenon sits humbly at the entrance in his black cassock. A simple carved wooden cross around his grey bearded neck catches the shade of his black kamilavkion on his head and of the old, parasol attached to a small table of souvenirs displaying mugs with crucifixes, bowls of plastic miniature baby Jesus made in China, black woven crosses on woven cords, cheap gilded icons, faded tour guides and dog-eared post cards. He waits, like penitent people do, for the tourists to arrive. There are never many but the first today are Grace and Christian Houseman-Sweaty-Smith.

Allen, having completely emptied his sacks like Santa on a white Christmas, is in one of the finest mood he has ever been. His blood pressure shows slight hypertension on the monitor but he's not surprised after last night's action. More importantly his brain feels fucking marvellous. Light, refreshed, renewed even, and no erectile dysfunction. Penne finishes the bacon which they ate with poached eggs on the balcony next to Russell.

All is well, all is bliss, and Allen is genuinely happy for once. To make matters better, it is his day off and he plans to spend it in the best way he can, with Penne, his Bic razors and squirty cream. When the phone rings, snapping Allen out of his ideal fantasy, the name of the Devil flashes across the screen.

'Shit, buggery crap, buggery crap, shit, shite, bollocks!' Allen contains himself and answers the phone with false contentment. 'Hello Mrs Houseman-Smith, what may I do for you?'

'We've broke down in that knacker of a Jeep, well, the pissing tyres burst on these wanky roads.'

'So it's just the tyre then, not the rest of the vehicle?'

'Yeah, there's a huge tear in it and part of it has fallen off, it looks like an aubergine. Christian's tried to av a go but he's shit at anything like this. Anyway we can't find the bloody Jack or that bolt thingy. The rental place should be called Mystery Cars rather than friggin' Fantasy Cars.'

'Have you tried calling Fantasy?'

'No, I fucking ain't cos all the info and insurance is back at the villa wiv the contact numbers.' How clever.

'Where exactly are you?'

'We're on that fucking hill jus' below the monastery church thing. We're walkin' the rest of the way. Looks like it's only bout five hundred yards but it's bleedin hot and I'm in a bikini and heels.'

Christ, Father Basil isn't going to like that.

'I'll ring Fantasy for spares, and Niko, and I will be up there shortly. Just hang on and if you get to the monastery, be polite.' He cautions.

'Wot you mean Alleeeen, am always polite!'

'All in a day's work.' Allen explains to Penne, who is looking forward to a private beach day with Allen and possibly a barbecue.

'But you are not meant to be working today, mon cher!' Penelope is clearly disappointed, but she grudgingly understands after he faithfully tries to explain and promises that their plans for the day will happen, just a day late. As Allen turns to leave, Russell drops a lemon.

He calls Fantasy Cars then Nikos, who isn't overjoyed to receive a call from Allen. 'It's my day off, man!'

'Yeah, mine too, but I need your help.'

'Can't Fantasy sort this crap out? It's their *patisame* Jeep.'

'Well, yes, under normal circumstances they could, but unfortunately they have other mechanical breakdowns to sort out. Please don't swear at me in Greek.'

'Why not call the fucking place Reality Cars then?'

'Look, I've picked up a spare tyre and a lug wrench, you going to help or what?'

'Fine, pick me up in ten minutes.'

'Thanks buddy!' Allen replies gratefully.

15
Rescue one

The Hellenic Police pass Allen's Laskarina transit just before he turns onto the dirt track that leads to the monastery. The police car takes the same turn ahead of him. *Oh Fuck...* Allen and Nikos slowly follow the dust trail made by the blue and white car when another police car overtakes Allen's pottering wagon at some speed. Slowly, the dust settles ahead of them, allowing Allen and Nikos to see the discarded Jeep at the side of the road halfway up the hill. Allen is surprised Grace has thought about switching the Jeep's hazard lights on. They continue past the Jeep, climbing closer to the Monastery of Panagia Kastriani.

'They ain't going up there to find the Virgin Mary.' *Just Grace and Christian. It's amusing how ecclesiastical their names are,* Allen thinks.

They pull up by the Housemans' fantasy Jeep. Sure enough it has a flat tyre on the front driver's side. Grace was right, it was shredded, they must have continued to drive with the fucker like that for a bit. *Stupid bastards!* Thankfully, the trim looks intact. The keys are still in the ignition and what appears to be half of Grace's wardrobe on the back seat. *Well, it ain't going anywhere, so there's no need for Nikos to do some hot wiring.* Not to Grace's clothes, which judging by the state of them, should be burnt anyway.

Nikos loosens the bolts, jacks up the Jeep and fits the replacement tyre. Allen observes the police approaching from the monastery at great speed. The blue and white lights are still on and the cars show no sign of slowing down. It passes the repaired Houseman's Jeep and the transit. Through the road dust which has blown upwards due to the acceleration, Allen notices Grace through the back window, handcuffed, one boob hanging out of her bikini, with an equally handcuffed and no longer smoking Christian seated next to her. Grace seemed to be shouting something at Allen about Jesus.

Allen looks at Nikos, Nikos looks at Allen.

'Loulida' They say simultaneously.

'You want the van or the Jeep?'

'Jeep,' answers Nikos. 'Follow me, I know where the Police Station is.'

'As do I,' admits Allen drifting back to his amateur archaeology arrest. He wonders if they still have his pink air bed.

16
Loulida Hellenic Police

The police station on Kea is an intimate yet grim place. There is little crime on the island, apart from imported tourist stuff, road traffic accidents mostly involving mopeds, again caused by tourists, and the occasional historic, in-bred land dispute. Certainly no international crime syndicates or even Interpol required connections or, for that matter, British Embassy involvement in Athens. There are just two officers, Dikaios Vassos and Titus Spiros, who it should be stated are both good men, now looking very bored and are not relishing the prospect of all the ensuing paperwork.

'So what have they exactly done, Dikaios? Are they in real deep shit?'

Dikaios, a name given to Old Testament holy men, strokes his ginger stubbly chin and considers before responding.

'It is a difficult situation… How about, gross indecency, assault and desecration of a place of worship, to start off with?'

'So… not much then?' Allen tries to make light of the situation but fails. 'Where are they?'

'Giving statements to my colleague Titus Spiros.'

Titos and Dikos. Allen has an unexpected flashback to the lovely lady boy Cora Evangeline Roma in Athens.

'Can you tell me what they've done? Believe me, I appreciate they are fucking hard work, but they are my clients.'

'I can tell you nothing. Now I would refrain from swearing at me or you will be joining them.' Dikaios adjusts his cap to a jaunty angle.

'Come on, Dikaios, man, we go way back. Remember my airbed adventure? Surely there's some agreement can be made to sort all parties and avoid all the wretched paperwork. I'm sure it's a pain involving the British Embassy and solicitors. Plus, I believe the Housemans are quite wealthy.'

'Are you trying to bribe a police officer, Allen Mason Freeman? Note the "free man" part of your name right now.'

Allen holds his hands up in a gesture of submission. 'No, sir.'

'Good,' says Dikaios. 'Now, this is what happened. We get the call from Father Basil at Panagia Kastri, he is most disturbed, saying he has been assaulted and that the monastery has been vandalised and violated…'

The sentence is left suspended as Grace appears in another pink bikini top, micro shorts and matching handcuffs, escorted by Titus.

'I only got mi tits out, Alleeeen and gave the silly fucker a free view. I paid good money for 'em, may as well show the beauties off!'

Allen begins to realise the severity of their arrest. He sighs.

'Yes, but a monastery is a very inappropriate place to exhibit your naked breasts, particularly in front of a man of the cloth!'

'Well, that's the bleedin problem innit. He wanted me to cover up wiv some smelly old rugs or something. I ain't having that! God created me in this pissing image. Alright the tits have a bit of silicon stuffing in them but I ain't wearing someone's old rug when it's fecking hot as hell!'

'Apparently you assaulted him Mrs Houseman.'

'All I did was jus' knock his silly black hat off! Oh and take a baby Jesus out of his pot but I was going to pay, I promise! But the feds here arrested me before Christian could get his wallet out.'

'Christian threw a lit cigar into the holy font,' said Titus Spiros helpfully.

'He thought it was a fucking well, it was bleedin outside after all!'

'You don't drink cigars, Mrs Houseman, holy water or not!'

'Look, Allen, don't get cocky wiv me! If I get mi tits out I ain't so different as the Virgin sodding Mary, there are plenty of pics of her out there with the old jugs on display and baby Jesus hanging off em! They've even got one inside the bloody monastery, it's on the pissing ceiling!'

Allen was growing tired of Grace's theatrics, feeling the first signs of a combined high blood pressure and oncoming panic attack. He wished he were back in Penne's arms. He feels well fucking anxious, he needs to take his pills. The medication controls the severity of the attacks but does not cure or stop the cause of his irregular personal turmoil. He often sees the black dog, as he calls it, same as that famous fantastic Welsh poet. The dog watches him through the long grass of some imagined meadow, buttercups, dandelions and all, in some imagined land. Sometimes the dog is far away, almost unseen, but stalking him just the same. Sometimes the animal is nowhere to be seen, and sometimes it is so close he can see its bared, snarling teeth and the whites of its angry eyes. He remembers one of Anthony's poems.

Fear

Fear knocked loud and hard on the aged oak door.
Inside, comforted by the warmth from the fire,
Faith turned to Hope and asked hesitantly:
'Which of us will answer the door?'
Hope considered for a moment.
'We will answer it together, brother,' he replied,
'for we are now and ever after united in our purpose.'
So, Lo, they cast open the door wide.
And Fear was nowhere to be seen, heard, or felt at all.

'Alleeeeen! Wake up, grow a fucking pair and get us the fuck out of here!'

Allen looks at Dikaios, the holy policeman, who looks at Allen with sympathy. 'How much?' He asks with direct diplomacy, his panic attack partially repressed. Titus shrugs and looks at Dikaios.

'Father Basil would settle for a good donation.'

'What, blood?' Interrupts Grace.

'Shut up, you silly English fool!' Titus now looks angry. 'The Virgin's roof at the monastery needs fixing and our time is precious, one hundred and fifty thousand drachmas. One hundred for the priest, and fifty for us. We can get this shithole painted for that price.'

Dikaios looks at the decaying green paintwork. 'What do you think Titus? Pastel pink?'

'I'll get Christian,' says Titus. 'He's asleep. We do prefer American dollars though.'

'I might just as well be a virgin with the amount of sex Christian gives me! This is fucking extortion.'

'Shut up, Grace, for God's sake! Or spend the rest of your holiday in here!'

'Fair comment,' admits Grace, 'but call me Mrs Houseman, Allen. I'll be writing a review on this, and you'll be in the shit.'

17
Penne and Picnics

With the ransom paid, the Housemans home, and the Jeep restored and parked up outside their villa, Allen can finally enjoy his day off. The beach barbecue is on, the boat is fuelled and moored. He has taken his medication and finished the potato salad with a hint of chive and red onion, which he then places in the cooler with a bag of ice alongside a few bottles of local white wine, two steaks, which he has been assured are beef and not goat, two chicken souvlaki with onion and peppers, a bottle of water, two glasses, paper plates, plastic cutlery and a small bottle of brandy, which is mainly included to kindle the barbecue if Allen can't get 'the fucker to light'. Next to the cooler, Allen places two stolen Laskarina robes, two large white bath towels, a tartan rug made in South Korea and a Laskarina parasol. Allen has decided to take Penne to the most private of private beaches that he knows, called Psathi. The roads to this beach are impregnable, truly terrifying up to Orkos beach, its nearest neighbour. From there, the road diminishes into a mere track. There are no facilities, no bars, nothing but cobalt blue sea and a stone barbecue. Much to Allen's delight, he remembers from his previous adventure to Psathi that the paradise beach has no phone signal.

Allen dresses in all white, which brings out his tan. He isn't wearing his glasses so he can't really be sure, but he thinks he looks cool. Penne, however, he knows looks hot even with his restricted sight. Her Latino skin tone and jet-black bobbed hair is paired with fitted shorts that look like they've been sprayed on and a tight white vest top which reads 'Fuck It' in black across her breasts.

'Subtle,' Allen comments, admiring the top and the pert protruding nipples.

'Just giving you a few useful hints after yesterday's crap, sex doll.'

'Point number one taken, splice the main brace, hoist the jib sail, walk the plank or give me a wank.' Allen winks and starts the motor in one smooth pull action. Penne laughs, it's just all going so beautifully well.

18
Penne and Psathi

HMHS Britannic was the third and final vessel of the ill-fated White Star Line, commissioned to Harland & Wolff in Belfast. She was launched on the twenty-sixth of February 1914, and was the sister ship of the *RMS Titanic*. The Royal Navy operated her at the start of the First World War until she sank off Kea after hitting a German mine on the twenty-first of November 1916. At the time, *Britannic* was in service as a hospital ship operating between the UK and the Dardanelles. It only took fifty-five minutes for the vessel to sink, killing thirty out of the one thousand and sixty people on board. Along with their dire loss and the subsequent difficult rescue of the unfortunate souls left, there was reputed to be a substantial consignment of pure quality gold bullion to assist the British War effort. She is the largest ocean liner ever to have sunk and the wreck was explored by the legendary Jacques Yves Cousteau in 1975. Whilst Jacques found the wreck, the whereabouts of the gold remains undiscovered.

Allen successfully navigates the boat to Psathi beach. It was a simple operation, merely following the coastline and remembering to avoid the submerged rocks. He moors without difficulty on the isolated bay. The sand is coarse here but very white, causing the water to fluoresce bright blue when caressed by the sun. The bay itself is fringed by small, stunted pine and cypress trees in the foreground, with cliffs to the left, right and back. Allen can see his small stone-built barbecue still intact with its rusty griddle. He carries Penne through the waist-high water in a cross between the Heimlich manoeuvre and an intimate embrace, then wades back to the boat to retrieve the rest of their things. A slight breeze blows the parasol, threatening to topple him or provide a bit of improvised wind surfing.

'Right baby girl, you set up and I'll find some wood for the barbie.' Allen tries to do an Aussie accent, which is frankly lost on Penne.

'This is so beautiful, *mon cher*.' She says dreamily. 'Do you bring all your girls here?'

'I only got you, babe.' Allen shouts back, foraging below the tree line. He thinks about Chrissie Hynde and UB40's version. *Music! That's what I forgot to bring!*

Whilst the steaks and souvlakis are cooking and half a bottle of wine has been drunk, Penne and Allen enjoy an extravagant pre-lunch starter shag. Although Allen can't help but worry about the sand chaffing their intimates, the steaks overcooking, and the sudden realisation that there are two white beanie hats perched on two seated figures on the cliff edge to the left, watching. *The fucking intrepid, crazy Crawfords with their easels and all!*

Denholm has got his binoculars on Penne's sandy fabulous body. She lets out a very vocal orgasm.

'Ahoy, Allen. Don't mind us!' Margaritte Crawford shouts in a very English sort of way. 'We're off that way for a bit of painting and who knows what else, judging by your performance!'

Denholm keeps his focus on Penne through the binoculars as they depart, beanies bobbing over the headline, unlike Allen who now has a sagging erection.

'Great potato salad,' says the satisfied Penne. 'Are there any sausages?' She giggles, pointing to Allen's own bush line.

'If you peel it, you can eat it.' Allen says rather crudely, thinking about a quote he had heard somewhere before about wooden apples. 'Are you finished? There's some steak left.' He points to the barbecue.

'I certainly have, babe,' confirms Penne. 'I love a good bit of red meat. Now I need a swim, followed by some oral and a fuck from behind.'

'Happy to oblige.' He salutes both with his hand and his cock as he scans the cliff line for the beanie hats.

The sea is warm, but Allen and Penne spend a lot of their time in an embrace. Allen can only partially penetrate Penne, something reasonably difficult to accomplish in the sea when one has had a bottle of white and a swig or two of the brandy. After only slight success, they relocate to the comparative comfort of the Korean tartan rug and the shade from the parasol. The sex is fantastic, the wine is fantastic but sadly now all gone, and the brandy sends them both to sleep in the mid-afternoon sun.

When he wakes with a start, Penne still blissfully asleep in a prone stark naked position, he notices a pair of flippers attached to a scuba suit standing above him.

'Nice view!' Says the vaguely familiar but unrecognisable goggled face with back-strapped oxygen tanks.

'Stop looking at her!' Orders Allen, chucking a robe over Penne, who wakes badly and shouts, 'What the fuck!'

'I wasn't looking at her,' says the masked man staring at Allen's naked groin. It's fucking Finn Thompson, the gay marine. 'Nice sausage.' Allen covers his modesty with a towel.

'What can I do for you, Mr Thompson?' Allen smiles, trying to salvage his dignity in an unsalvageable situation.

'Nothing. It's more what I can do for you.' The flying Finn, or rather flippered Finn, pauses, admiring the view. Allen envisages various unpleasant sexual scenarios. 'Look down the beach,' orders Finn, 'and tell me what you see.' Allen looks down the beach, trying not to sound too flippant.

'Well the sky, the sand, the sea… Sweet Jesus! Where's our fucking boat gone?'

'Calm down, buddy!' Finn says like a marine in complete control. 'Big Al salvaged your boat around the headland. It obviously slipped its ropes when you were otherwise engaged.' Removing his goggles, he winks at him, then raises a Roger Moore eyebrow.

'Oh hiya,' Penne finally recognises Finn. She holds out a hand whilst trying to conceal her body. 'Lovely to see you again! Would you like some steak, we've got some left?'

'I've seen quite enough meat for one day, but is any of that brandy on offer?'

Allen hands him the bottle. 'You want a glass?'

'Allen, I may be gay but I ain't no puff. Alistair is towing your boat back, it's attached to ours. I like your action, buddy, for an old un you still got some good moves.'

Allen and Penne change put on their robes and swimwear whilst Finn politely faces in the other direction. The whole situation is becoming an episode of 'Miami Vice' as Big Al majestically walks up the beach towards them, equally flippered after having secured Allen's boat.

'Any of that brandy left?' Alistair asks Finn when he is in earshot.

'Sure bro!' Finn screws the top back on and chucks it at his brother, who sublimely catches it with one hand and unscrews the cap in one seamless movement.

'So that explains the case.'

'Yep. We're wreck-diving over to the south there. Lucky for you, we saw your boat drifting.' Allen can't figure out whether it is the brandy or the sight of Allen's cock that has made Finn more communicative.

'Thanks buddy. We'd be fucked here without a boat, there's no way off land otherwise.'

'Looks like you've been well fucked anyway.'

'Good observation,' says Penne.

Allen tactfully changes the subject. 'So, you're looking for the gold on the *Britannic* I assume.' Finn cautiously stares at Allen.

'So you know the story.'

'Yeah, I like history and archaeology. Although not the marine type, dry land for me.'

'Clearly. With your boating skills I'm surprised you didn't drown getting here.'

Allen purposefully ignores Alistair.

'You know, I think it's a registered war grave.'

'Probably,' admits Finn, 'but we've got permits. It's a Brit ship and we're part of the Royal Marines. Now, any more questions and I'll have to shoot you.'

Penne is clearly alarmed.

'He's only joking,' says Alistair. It seems to relieve her but Allen isn't sure the relief is somewhat misplaced.

'You ready to leave? There's a slight chop to the sea, we will escort you both back to the harbour, we are on our way there anyway to pick up some supplies.'

'Thanks bud. Let us just get our shit together and dowse the barbecue.'

The journey back to Korissia is uneventful. Allen follows Finn and Big Al in their inflatable marine craft. Penne is at the front, sitting like a goddess without her breasts out. Finn and Al dock first and help Allen with his gear, which he thanks them for.

'Seriously guys, thanks a million, I'm in your debt! I hope you find the gold. If you do, send Penne a bar, one for me and Nikos too.' They all laugh.

On their way back to the bakery flat, Allen notices all Mateo's goats have escaped again and are kidding around by the pool next to Anthony's apartment. He turns his phone back on to alert Mateo and notices twelve missed calls from Grace. *Fuck that.* After speaking to Mateo, he turns the phone back off. *Mañana*, he thinks.

19
In with the Gecko

Hemidactylus turcicus, more commonly known as the Mediterranean house Gecko, gets its name from where its name suggests, Gecko. They bask on the stone walls and on occasion venture inside the home for a break from the sun, to seek water or just have a brief holiday. In this case, "brief" being the operative word. However, they are not generally known to be panty-sniffers and usually not to be found in a woman's knicker drawer. Why is it that our undergarments are always found in the top drawer of a chest of drawers?

Allen leaves Penne sleeping with a hastily written invitation to dinner at Dimitri's Fish Taverna later. He wedges it under the Art Nouveau lamp, with lots of kisses for her. Allen calls the Devil, knowing he can't ignore the all-powerful-who-must-be-obeyed Grace Houseman-Smith. As usual, the phone rings once before her grinding voice answers.

'Alleeeen, where the fuck you been? I could be dead or summat!'

I sometimes wish you were… 'Sorry Mrs Houseman-Smith, I missed your call yesterday.'

'No, you missed bleedin' twelve of em! Now to me that sounds gross neglect and desecration of duty.' *Dereliction*, thinks Allen, but he doesn't correct her and continues to listen to the ensuing tirade. 'Look, one miss' call is a fucking mistake okay, two is just careless, three could be an accident, but four is jus' taking the piss!'

God knows what twelve is, *Sodom and Gomorrah maybe? Certainly something Hieronymus Bosch could paint or even a plague of biblical bloody locusts.* 'Sorry, Mrs Houseman, had some family business to attend to. A bereavement.'

'I don't care,' answers Grace with her usual compassion. 'All I want sorted is mi trip to the Owacle and some advice about bites. I put some panties on out mi knicker drawer yesterday and felt something wriggling around in em, it was a bleedin lizard! Now I've just shaved mi bush and the fucker bit my clit on its way out! Could I die? Do I need medical attention?'

He tries to suppress a laugh which slips out as a strangled cough. *Not your clit, your brain probably ... you must have a big bit of gear though for it to find that.* Allen shakes his head, trying to remove the thought from his wandering mind. 'Where is the thing now?'

'What, mi clit? In the same bleedin' place.'

'No, the gecko.'

'The what? Oh, you in "Dad's Army". I saw the shows, you know.'

'The lizard!'

'Oh, Christian hit it with a flip flop, and it pissed off under the bed.' Allen subconsciously imagines the strange scene of Christian hitting the unfortunate gecko and Grace's clit at the same time with a plastic sandal. An unpleasant thought really, certainly Elvis would have a comment or two about it.

'Your lower regions will be fine, are they ... swollen?' Allen is doubled over, silently laughing. Its Grace's sanity he worries about.

'I ain't telling you if I've got a swollen clit you perv.'

He composes himself. 'Look, Mrs Houseman, you'll be fine, this is Greece after all. I'll call you later when I've spoken to Yannis about the Oracle trip.' Allen should have ended the call but he couldn't resist. 'Get Christian to put some cream on it but not taramasalata again.' He promptly ends the call and collapses to the ground in hysterics.

'You okay?' Nikos asks cautiously. 'You are not having a stroke or anything?' Allen carries on laughing.

Allen catches his breath finally. 'No I'm fine, dear friend.'

'You coming to Mateo's then? We get some breakfast for a change.' Allen brushes himself down as he stands up. 'Sure. I've got a story to tell, and you'll love this one.'

20
Breakfast at the Windy Bar

'You will lose those goats, Mateo, if you don't fix that crap gate.' Comments Allen, seated with the poet Anthony, Nikos and three large breakfast club sandwiches. Mateo just shrugs.

'So? I don't like the bastards anyway. Enjoy.'

Mateo's breakfast club sandwiches are the best, but nothing like a proper club sandwich should be. The calorific value in one alone would be enough to feed a starving person for two days. Chorizo, sliced and wedged between thick local bread with fried eggs, bacon, and chewy cheese, the stuff that comes individually wrapped in multipacks with radically concealed opening instructions. There's not a hint of salad in sight.

'I'll have an Ouzo, a large one, with mine, *efharisto*'. Anthony enquires.

'Bit early for that don't you think?'

'Bugger off! I'm on holiday, an alcoholic, a poet and proud of it.' Allen submits with outstretched arms. They finish their sandwiches in silence and Anthony gets his morning shot of Ouzo.

'Bloody good that!' Anthony says in relief, breaking the silence. 'Almost as tasty as that girl of yours, Allen. I imagine she's sweet as a peach. Where did you find her?'

'Athens.'

'Well, she is a goddess, a real fox as we old public school boys would say. I drink to forget my name, you know. I wrote a poem once about a fox want to hear it?'

Even the Pope couldn't stop him or make him forget it.

Fox

Run red, run, brave vixen fox,
run red, run with me.
To the click of the gate, the quick go free,
run, red fox, with me.

Anthony coughs. The first hit of Ouzo making its mark. 'Sorry gents.'

Run, red fox, past the waiting yew,
and the form in the rags,
with scythe sharpened true.
Run, red fox, with me.

Run, vixen fox,
run fast and light.
Through the waving corn
Of the Lamma's night.
Run, sweet fox, with me.

Run, fox, run,
Past the stone on the hill,
That stands alone,
ancient and still.
Run, fox, run with me.

Run, red, run
To where the ferry man waits,
At the water's edge,
for the gilded gates.
Run, red, but slow your pace.

Let us run as one,
for this is no race.

'Do you think I should have called that "Red" rather than "Fox"?

Am not so good with titles.' Anthony takes another slurp of Ouzo. 'Anyone seen the bloody bowl of ice to go with this?'

'Another magnum opus,' adds Allen.

'You can only have one of those I believe, dear boy, but thank you all the same.'

'Truly great work.' Nikos adds. Anthony beams in a modest, sanguine drunk sort of way whilst Allen takes out the phone to ring Yannis before the Devil bothers him with more of her badgering.

'Yannis, mate, ringing about the trips, where we at?'

'We are at the point that I hit you over the head with this heavy wrench or, if you prefer, a lump hammer,' replies Yannis. 'I am covered head to toe in fucking oil! I look like a dolma or a bastard seal, and I'm not talking the American navy here. I am trying with my colleagues to fix this big twat of a boat to get your weirdoes to the Oracle in Delphi. The small shit ship for the usual Karthea cruise is fine and will happen the day after tomorrow. Tell your clients I have the booze, the staff and the stuff for the bloody beach barbecue at Vroskopos sorted. Tell the Oracle the trip will be in three days, departing from the harbour at seven, okay? Now piss off and let me fix this bastard thing.' He ends the call.

'Well that's me told.' Allen orders a Campari with ice and a small Greek coffee from Mateo.

21
DIMITRI'S FISH BAR

'Do you have fresh lobsters?'

'We do,' replies Dimitri, 'they are in the tank over there, but it is expensive.'

'I really don't give a sod,' admits Allen, 'and don't patronize me whilst I'm entertaining,' he jokes. 'Just do us two of your best lobster Thermidors with some skinny fries and a green salad and all served at the same time, please.'

'You're the boss.' Dimitri wanders off.

Allen looks at Penne, a vision in a Karen Millen silk little black dress with wavy pleats and ankle-length pointed stiletto boots. Allen is wearing a black cotton Mandarin Kenzo suit with a Nehru collar. He feels like James Bond, although a mature version, more late Sean Connery than early Roger Moore. He orders a bottle of Bollinger, which impresses both Penne and Dimitri. The taverna is beautifully set, located slightly higher than the adjacent ground to obtain fine views of the Bay of St Nicholas and the natural topiary bay balls in pots. The tables are set with pristine white linen tablecloths around the pots and olive trees. The trees bear fruits and are adorned with a plethora of white fairy lights that look like fireflies. Their conversation is fine, easy, and lovingly mellow. The lobsters, which Allen had preselected from the tank at the back of the restaurant, soon arrive. A horrible process, like playing Russian roulette with the poor beasts' lives. He had pointed at the fate of two unfortunate lobsters and given Dimitri a small box. 'You know where to put it, right? Just don't cook it or bloody lose it.' Dimitri had nodded. Allen loves Thermidor almost as much as he loves Penne, but he hasn't told her yet.

The Thermidor, salad, and the skinny fries arrive with the assistance of Callista and Helena, Dimitri's waitresses. The plates are topped with sparklers, making the other guests look. Something else, even sparklier, is wedged between the lobster's right claw.

'Be careful with that one, it's rather special,' Dimitri says, serving

Penne, with a wink.

'Ooh, this looks fabulous!' Comments Penne, not noticing Mr Lobster's claw. She nearly covers it in *insalata verde* and Allen tries to move it slightly with his lobster fork.

'Hey, get off my lobster, you bitch!' Says Penne, moving the now dead sparklers and noticing something else still sparkling. Allen's phone rings with all the timing of a dead fish. It's the Devil.

'Yes, yes, yes!' She cries, busting the lobster claw off in her eagerness to retrieve the ring, which she promptly drops on top of Allen's head. He is now kneeling in front of her, wearing some lettuce, a slice of green pepper, and some red onion. His phone still ringing, Dimitri and the other dinner guests are already applauding.

'Hold on, hold on! I ain't asked her yet.' Allen shouts above the noise.

'I really don't think you need to.' Dimitri beams as the frantically clapping Callista and Helena, and Theo the chef, get caught up in the moment and throw a few empty plates around the room.

'This one's on me, buddy.' Whispers Dimitri.

'You're a good man.' Allen chucks his ringing phone into the nearest bay tree pot. He grabs Penne's hand.

'You do like lobster, don't you? And oh! Would you like to marry me?' He proposes, almost as an afterthought.

The ensuing party is fantastic, even Saffron and Kevin turned up for some impromptu Greek dancing, along with the elusive gardener Bret from south Derbyshire. He strangely has further facial injuries, which he says are plant-inspired while chucking some plates with vigour. The Crawfords appear too, still in the same beanie hats, still drinking gin but not dancing.

'After your performance on that beach the other day, I'm not surprised. A match made in heaven, I'd say.' Denholm Crawford whispers confidentially to Allen.

Mateo arrives to join the fun, pushing a completely shit-faced poet in his faulty chair. The Thompsons are missing, not just in action, but in attendance too, as are the How-How-Hateful-Housemans, thankfully. Grace's calls go unanswered on Allen's mobile phone below the bay foliage in terracotta pot number four, along with a sour cocktail that Saffy didn't like. Later, Kevin informs them all that the Karthea boat trip is on, with barbecue and leisure to swim in the blue water lagoon. Whilst receiving the information, Allen notices Bret eyeing up Saffron.

'Do we need to bring anything, Allen?'

'No, just swimwear and some sensible shoes.'

'Well, I'm coming too,' adds Bret, still looking at Saffy, no doubt thinking about swimwear. 'Is that okay, Allen?'

'Absolutely!'

22
Haircare

'You could try Anastasia Hair and Beauty?'

'Anaesthetic, hair and beauty?' Grace yelps.

Christ, I wish I had some! I'd put you flat out for the next week and a half. 'No, Mrs Houseman, *Anastasia*. 'It means sort of resurrection in Greek.'

'What's that?'

'It's what happened to Jesus when he rose from the dead.'

'Bit harsh for a hairdresser's innit, Allen. And why didn't you answer your bleedin phone last night, I could av booked it wiv em then?'

'I was getting engaged,' adds Allen dryly. 'I assume you know what that is, when two people love each other and plan to spend the rest of their lives together.'

'Fuck me, Alleeeen,' *No thanks,* 'after twelve years with Christian I wish I'd never accepted. Although the money ain't bad I suppose, but the guy's an utter twat. Anyway, I need mi roots doing.'

You need more than that sorting, thinks Allen. *Roots severed at the neck possibly.*

As with many Hellenic islands, scabby cats and feral strays are all part of the Greek experience. It is mainly the tourists fault. They decide to feed the unfortunate creatures, only to piss off home after a period of two weeks, leaving the cats to starve or the new residents to take up their responsibility. On the tourist cat-feeding European chart, the Brits normally score a prestigious ten whilst the Germans enter in at a modest two. Some Brits feed the cats so much that entire restaurants are required to close due to extreme pussy infestation, and not just sea food or even crabs here. Wave after wave of vicious feline muggers who steal the customers' calamari when they aren't looking, and claw at their shins when they are. The Anastasia Hair and Beauty clinic was unfortunately no exception.

Grace arrives at 5pm, shortly after the siesta. Unfortunately, the local cats, as usual, have not been fed, therefore there is a slight frenzy to their behaviour as they hover around the black steel, and very modern, chrome entrance door to the salon. As she enters, she traps one unfortunate cat in the door, a mishmash of colours with oddly orange ears. It screeches at Grace and runs off. Arianna escorts Grace politely to a chair and pours her a pink prosecco.

'Aww thanks bird. I jus' want mi blonde roots doing, well they ain't blonde if you follow me and that's the point.'

'No problem,' assures Arianna. 'Please sit and wait a few moments. Put your water you're holding on the station in front of the mirror.' Grace follows through with Arianna's instructions then sits back and enjoys her wine. What Arianna doesn't know is that Grace has already been drinking and a further glass of prosecco might perhaps be a tad optimistic in the sobriety stakes. Particularly on top of the rather large seafood lunch she has previously consumed. In truth, Grace feels a little nauseous. Arianna returns with a small black bowl of mixed bleach and peroxide, and two large dark chocolates, which Grace declines but places on the hair station in front of her alongside the now opened water. Arianna applies the chemicals to Grace's head with a small tinting brush and attempts a conversation.

The timing of this hair procedure and what occurs next is crucial. The salon has another customer, an elderly lady who has just had, and by now paid for, a wash and set. Grace's uneaten chocolates, coupled with the now fully applied and unpleasant smelling peroxide mix, are really starting to play havoc with her digestive system. Even more so when the heat from the five-spot infrared heat lamp is switched on. The entire process was like some form of virtual domino effect to Grace. Bleach, essentially chlorine dissolved in water, is not a flammable substance on its own; however, if mixed with certain agents, in this case ammonia or peroxide, it can become unstable to form an explosive compound.

As the elderly lady exits the salon, one young, thin, unhappy cat with orange ears enters unseen. The cat wastes no time and jumps onto Grace's hair station to grab the chocolates. Grace screams in shock under the lamp, throwing up over the cat, who forgets about the chocolates and instead focuses on Grace's processed seafood. The cat, in its distracted attention, accidentally knocks the near-full litre bottle of water over with its tail. The liquid spills at a remarkable speed to the electrics, causing the salon's main fuse board to blow, the lights to go off and the heat lamp to explode over Grace's peroxided head, into a small fire.

'Oh no!' There are so many no's gushing from Arianna's mouth it could make a good drum and bass track. 'We are so, so, sorry.'

She sprays the confused Grace with the shower head connected to the wash basin.

'This isn't too hot, is it?'

'Look, lady, you've almost blown mi head off!'

Arianna continues to spray Grace with water to remove the peroxide, dispersing the sick and broken glass from the bulb to quell any further possibility of fire.

Grace, in shock, whines. 'I know I wanted mi bleedin' roots doing but this is just fucking ridiculous! I ain't got any roots left to fucking bleach.'

Someone manages to unplug the lamp, get the power back on, and kick the cat out of the front door. It struts off to create chaos elsewhere and no doubt have a sick removing facial. Arianna surveys Grace's new hairstyle, which affords a Grace Jones meets Tom Jones impression. She picks up her mobile phone and calls Allen, whom she has right at the very top of her contacts list.

'Alleeeen!' She shouts as soon as he answers. 'They've fucked part of mi hair off! There's been one big accident, and where there's a blame there's a claim, right?'

Oh sweet Lord what have I done to deserve this. 'Ruining people's hair isn't that what most hairdressers are supposed to do.'

When Grace leaves the salon, again looking sadly like a parody of the port, she smells of sick, with a hint of peroxide this time. She sports a sort of cobbled-together punk hairstyle far too young for her, but which she actually quite likes, although she certainly wouldn't admit it. The singed parts to the left of her hair line have been radically shorn, combed over and tidied with the clippers. What was left was all bleached blonde with a huge quiff that droops dramatically from the left of her head to the full length on the right. Grace appreciates the hairstyle but, most importantly, that it was free.

'Jus' hope the fecking wind don't blow or I'm going to look like some sad old cow losing her head scarf.' Grace mumbles. She knows Christian won't like her new style, which is why she likes it even more.

23
Vroskopos and Ancient Karthea

'All aboard for the Kea boat trip! We'll be sailing through the beautiful Vroskopos Bay and the ancient city of Karthea! An experience not to be missed or ever forgotten!' Allen booms like a proper tour guide should, atop the small boats Command Centre, manned by Yannis, who really has little to command. They don't even have a radio and God knows where the life jackets are.

They do, however have the essentials: wine, lagers, orange juice, ouzo for Anthony, who raises his Panama hat, and chicken souvlaki. Plus a few fresh fish with local lemons. So what could be better? The sun is out as ever, the sky is blue as ever, the ship, as ever, is a tarted up knacker—Allen doesn't mention this bit to his guests—, and Penne is here, wearing her engagement ring, which makes him truly happy. She looks great and, frankly, blows Saffron out to the water. *Possibly the wrong choice of words for a small sea cruise.* The water is a little choppy and Allen wonders exactly how he is going to get the wheeled poet off the boat at Karthea without a winch.

It was unknown whether it was the gentle sway of the boat, the previous day's seafood-peroxide mix or the perpetual sway of Anthony's brake-less chair that slowly rolled from aft to port which caused Grace to be sick again. Kevin had attempted to wedge the poet's wheelchair still with a cooler but it was only a temporary success. Instead of sensibly easing herself to the leeward side of the ship that faces away from the wind to throw up, Grace grabbed the other cooler box. The one containing the chilled wine, larger, ouzo, orange juice and ice.

'Nice…' Exclaims Kevin, twisting his face.

'How very rude.' Adds Denholm Crawford.

'Oh crap!' Allen shouts loudly, awaking a sunbathing Penne with such a start that her sunglasses fly off her head and fall off the boat, into the sea. Allen reaches for the hose and pump to douse Grace and the contents of the cooler, chucking the ice overboard intentionally and, accidentally, the corkscrew with it. The corkscrew, a particularly nice one, was naturally not made to float. Allen sluices out the cooler, the bottles, people's feet, and the decking, growing irritated.

'I'll buy you a new pair, hon, have these until then.' Allen hands his Ray-Ban Orbs, with gilded frames, to Penne, the best sunglasses known to man.

Meanwhile, Christian lights up another huge cigar. In the distance, somewhere to starboard right, Allen thinks he can see Finn, Alise, and the Marine inflatable. *Maybe they could find Penne's glasses and my fucking corkscrew*, he thinks.

Bret from Derbyshire, and large-breasted Gloucester Saffron, seem to be getting on a little too well for Kevin, muscle-bound Braintree or Brainless of Essex, it is all the same in Kevin's case. They are leaning towards each other, engaged in an entertaining conversation, no doubt about rhododendrons and peonies. Allen hopes for Kevin's sake that this is not what he inadvertently overheard them talking about.

'Vroskopos beach ahead!' Yannis shouts.

'Mine's a glass of sick white vino, what's yours Anthony?'

'Sick ouzo please,' replies the poet. 'Wrote a poem about sick, want to hear it?

No one has the chance to stop him.

'This isn't going to make poor Mrs Houseman-Smith, ill again, is it?' Allen warns.

'No dear boy,' replies the poet. 'It's called "Meat".'

Meat

Happy hour in party land,
flesh exposed more, wedged in tight.
Lycra girl all made up,
totters in high heels,
held fragile as a house of cards.
She skates the vomit on the pavement.

Grace wretches again. 'Soz,' she politely adds.

…
Vomit on the pavement then,
face lit by ruby neon and the strobing crystal blue,
at another pointless fight, in the market of the night.

And as the lost love sirens wail,
she takes it hard, pressed against the council bins—

Grace interrupts again. 'I've dun that!' Followed by a 'sorry.'

…
Against the council bins,
heels braced in a pool another left.
Flushed hot with glistening sweat,
panties offered to the floor,—

Allen coughs anxiously wondering, exactly where this is going.

…
Panties on the floor,
chlamydia- and testosterone-fused.
A cocktail of regret,
in small town UK,
something to forget,
happening outside your door.

'What is testosterone?' Enquires Yannis.

'Ask Bret,' growls Kevin, glaring at the scarred gardener from South Derbyshire, still chatting with Saffy.

'Hard hitting', reflects Allen.

'Reminds me of Athens,' adds Penne in a quiet voice much older than her young years.

Margaritte adjusts her beanie hat. 'Well, there's none of that in Tunbridge Wells, is there, Denholm? None of that at all, thank you very much.' She adamantly states.

Bret and Kevin, having reached some form of understanding about peonies, lift Anthony, in the chair with a flask, onto the small, rustic, and highly unsafe jetty. It is more like a few wooden planks attached to what appears to be converted cypress tree trunks held together in the water by gravity or flotation alone. Luckily, it is wide enough for the poet's chair and long enough for him to reach the beach. He gratefully waves his silver flask.

'Fancy a quick hit of ouzo for your efforts, boys? Good job I'm not a fat bastard, what ho! Please just dump me over there but not forever, mind! More in the shade, under that lovely, stunted pine.' He points at the tree with his monogrammed flask, which is sort of his pacemaker without the electrics.

The boys dump him there but decline the drink. They amble back to Yannis and Allen, chaperoning the Crawfords off the boat with their painting equipment along with the hampers. Saffron and Penne, meanwhile, dive gracefully from the boat, swimming like true mermaids to the beach. A sight of immense beauty that leaves the men to get their things alongside the girls', the equipment for the barbecue, one forgotten beanie, some firelighters and Allen's Ray-Ban Orbs.

Allen is the one to get the fire started. He gets the handmade barbecue, which is another of his beach-combing, previously-manufactured designs. He washes the griddle in the sea and gets out the fish whilst Grace attempts to lay some beach towels on the golden untrodden sand. Christian solely smokes his cigars as usual, but does manage to open a bottle of sick-covered local white wine by pushing the cork into the bottle like a true professional. The accompanying spray hits him in the eye and extinguishes his cigar.

'Bastard!' He grunts. 'Only got one left.'

'What? An eye or a brain, you bleedin' twat? Now give us a hand wiv these towels, will ya.'

The Crawfords set up to paint with their lightweight easels after commandeering a glass from Christian. Allen notices they have both brought their bottles of Schweppes Tonic, no doubt filled with a mix of gin, lemon juice and, of course, tonic. They should be all right and will probably be asleep by the time the boat reaches Karthea.

'Mmmm, something smells good!' Anthony shouts from the stunted pine tree. 'Any sausages on board? Wrote a poem about them once, sort of a tribute to American popular culture. Want to hear it?'

Oh Christ, not again!

'Fine, Anthony.' Allen responds. 'Just go ahead but keep it clean, understand?'

The poet clears his throat, swigs a giant slurp of ouzo, and shouts, 'I understand, Allen!'

Sausages

I am the original sausage man,
making my sausages as fast as I can.
From the poor little pups
I abduct in my van,
That's why they're called Hot Dogs.

'That's just sick!' Allen exclaims, but he fortunately is the only one to hear the poem as the rest of the group is out of earshot.

'Yes,' considers the poet, adjusting his spectacles. 'Maybe, but appropriate for a barbecue. It's sort of Roald Dahl meets Oscar Wilde on a drinking day. Wilde's poison was absinthe, mine's ouzo.'

'Fair comment,' replies Allen. 'The souvlaki is nearly cooked, or you can have a grilled fish, but no sausage at all, okay?'

The barbecue is a great success, and all seems to be back on plan. At the end, Kevin and Bret extinguish the embers in the usual British foul sort of way, then lug a severely drunk Anthony back on the boat.

'You need to get this brake fixed.' Bret says.

'I need to get a lot of things fixed!' Slurs the poet. 'But brakes are quite low on my to-do list at present. But thanks dear boy.'

Penne unties the mooring rope, coiling it like an expert in true cowboy style, and hurls it on board, jumping on in one smooth, graceful action. Grace has, by the look of her, already caught too much sun and shades her head with a spare bikini top that appears to be slightly singed just like her hair. The bikini cups give her a sort of Minnie Mouse look without the car or the skirt.

'To Karthea then!' Announces Yannis as he fires up the engine and adds a piratey "eeh haw mi hearties!" for good measure. He always does this on Allen's tours and Allen really wishes he wouldn't, because Kea isn't Cornwall.

But the Crawfords like it, and Denholm even adds, 'Splice the main brace, Captain!' Although at this point, Denholm is already quite spliced, judging by the almost empty Schweppes bottle.

'How long will this take?' Asks Christian, whose cigar supply is seriously running low.

Allen notices that both Bret and Kevin are sitting on the bow with an arm around Saffy's golden back, as hot as the sun, drinking larger.

'Hmm this could be interesting,' Allen whispers to Penne. He raises an eyebrow and cocks his shoulder in their direction.

'Would that be a first?' Penne smiles.

Allen considers, possibly a bit too long for Penelope's liking.

'Definitely!' He lies, 'but I did meet Hugh Cornwell and the Stranglers.'

24
Karthea and Hornets

'The ruins of the Acropolis, town centre and fortifications of ancient Karthea have been preserved for centuries on the Aspri Vigla hills. The Doric temple of the goddess Athena and the Temple of Pythion Apollo can be found here. You will be able to see them more clearly when we dock, but they are visible now,' Allen points in their direction, 'in the valley of Vathipotamos.'

'Hippopotamus, you say, are there some of them here?' Asks Margaritte, somewhat nervously.

'No. Vathipotamos is the location of the Temple of Demeter. There's also a first-century-BCE theatre there that's worth checking out.'

'So, what's showing?' Christian questions. 'Ben fucking Hur?'

'Very good,' says Allen like he hasn't heard the joke before. 'Demetra, Zeus's older sister, the goddess of Corn, and I'm not referring to humour here, but agriculture and farming.'

'Must have stopped raining years ago,' Bret interrupts helpfully, looking at the state of the place and the large number of prickly pears.

Anthony is off first, the same procedure as at Vroskopos beach. He looks at the hills and the rough track leading up to the temple.

'You won't get me to the top, fellas. It's just too much to ask. Just bung me on that promontory over there, where I can write my stuff and see the view. After all, one column is pretty much like any other really, unless it's MDF! I've seen a few columns in my time, believe me, but don't tell the Admiral! Not Yannis, I'm talking about Nelson here.'

Bret and Kevin, who seem to be bonding extremely well, heave the poet from the boat onto the small stone jetty. They alternate between pushing and dragging, and finally lift Anthony up the rough dirt track in the full heat of the sun, an arduous task that requires muscles. Greek historic sites are notorious for their lack of access. It seriously makes someone wonder how exactly they invented the chariot or, if they didn't invent the thing, how they used them so much to win wars. They plant Anthony under the shade of a huge cactus.

Allen wakes up Margaritte, who instantly grabs her watercolours and kicks Denholm in the ankle, also asleep and snoring lightly. Bret nudges Kevin while watching Allen deal with the other passengers on the boat.

'We really should give Allen our NI numbers for all this work.' Kevin takes a moment to process Bret's suggestion. 'Do you know what an NI is Kev?' Bret jokes.

'Sure,' he answers with a broad grin, 'No Idea or No ID.'

The Crawfords set up to paint some Doric columns. Grace drags Christian off the boat, who seems extremely eager to view the antiquities. This is all but a complete lie. The closest he likes being to ruins is next to Grace on a sun lounger at the villa. Bret finds his camera and one of those huge lenses to attach to the camera. With a thick Olympus strap, it is quite apt for the Greek history tour. He sets off up the hill with Saffy, Kevin, and a bottle of wine they have taken from the sick chiller.

As tranquillity returns, Penne and Allen take a brief swim and embrace in the crystal waters like two nymphs. *Well, one nymph accompanied by the Hulk, without the green tint and excessive muscle.* Yannis sits inside the boat, like Captain Birdseye minus the cap, tinkering with the engine, which is probably as old as Karthea itself.

An outrageous screech takes everyone by surprise. Bret, who is up by the columns taking topless pictures of Saffy—with Kevin's approval by the looks of things—, throws his camera at Kevin who, like a true Olympian athlete catches it in one take, as Bret charges down the hill. But as goddess Saffron pulls her top back on, he falls into a prickly pear cactus, something one should never do. He screams as one would whilst gingerly untangling himself from the barbed plant. He is soon up and out but with now a few more scars on his face and torso.

'Not to worry, I'm a gardener. I'm used to this sort of things. That's Grace, she's been stung on the ass by a hornet or a wasp, I'm just going to suck the poison or sting out.'

Brave man, thinks Allen, *there's a lot of poison in that ass.* The

Crawfords approach as well, two slightly gin-enhanced, avant-garde watercolours in hand.

'Ahoy!' They yell. 'We heard screams, is everyone okay?'

'Think so,' says Allen wondering if he's losing the plot. 'Bret is just sucking out Grace's ass.'

'Oh dear, how very unpleasant,' says Margaritte in a Royal Tunbridge Wells sort of way. 'I believe that's called "rimming".'

'She is going to need an antihistamine or some vodka. Maybe both.' Bret adds as they depart Karthea.

'Are we still diving?' Saffy asks dreamily, looking at the clear blue water.

'I certainly hope so,' says Kevin, looking at Bret, who is openly looking at Saffy bent over the gunwale. Despite his scratches, he certainly seems up for it.

'Grace will be fine, let's dive for a bit then take her to a doctor.' He said like any true medical professional.

'Anthony has already blitzed her with ouzo and, frankly, she's out of it.' Kevin observes.

'Thankfully not the bikini,' Bret states, somewhat relieved. 'I've applied an antiseptic and covered the wound. So, really, speaking as a qualified first aider, there isn't much we can do, she doesn't appear to be having any toxic reaction.'

'What about her husband, Christian?' Enquires Allen.

'Oh, I've been supplying him with some home grown weed. He's having his own toxic reaction and is as happy as Larry. Just don't let him go swimming.' Bret cautions them.

'I've always wondered who Larry actually was.' Allen whispers to Penne whilst swigging the last of the Mythos. 'Larry the Lamb, Larry Grayson, Larry the sodding Lion … Shit buggery shit! The Lion of Kea! I forgot to mention that one to the punters at the tour meet!'

The Lion of Kea is a colossal archaic sculpture of a guardian lion. What it is guarding, no one really knows. Perhaps someone should move it to see what is hidden underneath. It was sculpted sometime in the sixth century BCE. The big beast is not the best anatomically chiselled lion but highly spiritual nonetheless, cut from a block of limestone. Barbara Hepworth finds a large chunk of rock on a bad day with a chisel.

The dive site is in deep sea, around a rocky islet. The water is cooler there but still clear, beautiful yet warm enough to explore without wetsuits. The rock wall plunges forty meters below the surface, making it better suited for scuba diving, but the water still fluoresces that enticing vivid blue. A dream for snorkellers and mermaids.

Instead of expecting the dark below the wash of the waves, adventurers are met view a marvellous view. The clear water is fringed with numerous corals and sea creatures. Although not a reef, it is impressive and occupied with groupers, snappers, large tunas, and turtles. For Allen, however, the most impressive part of this particular dive occurs when Saffron loses her white string-tied, flimsy thong when she dives from Yannis the Captain's roof. The naturist theme is further entertained, much to Margaritte Crawford's disgust and Denholm's imperceptible amusement, when Kevin removes his matching white Speedos, exposing his member, akin in size to that of a small stallion. The whole scenario is topped with a true Brit bomber into the sea. Bret catches it, not literally Kevin's genitals, but an image of it on his camera, although the zoom was not needed on this occasion. Allen wonders how he gets that monster in a pair of Speedos. He shields Penne's eyes whilst considering his own girth.

'Fuck me, that's a big one!' Bret says.

Penne agrees, pushing Allen overboard so she can have a better view.

Christian wakes from a semi drug-induced coma. 'Anyone just seen those dolphins?'. He instantly re-joins Anthony in sleep, who has been out of it through the entire farce.

Yannis just shakes his head, 'You English are so weird…'

Bret, equally well-endowed and equally weird, turns to Denholm. 'No swimming I take it?'

'No, dear fellow, not for us. No snorkelling either, but the views are rather pleasant here.' He watches Saffy's beautiful naked ass resurface.

'Great. Could you hang on to my camera then? Don't get it wet.' He hands him his camera.

'Yannis has got all the snorkelling stuff out.' He points to the pile near the boat. 'No one has used it.'

'Sod that,' replies Bret, promptly removing his black surfing shorts in front of the beanie-hatted Margaritte. She looks away, appalled, as Bret dives in, shaven balls and naked over the boat's side.

At the end of the unintended naturist diving session, Yannis fires up the engine. Thankfully, all passengers are safe, partially-clothed and safely on board. He desperately wishes he could go home, dump the Brits, and consume a vast quantity of raki.

The dual props start to spin, but the boat unfortunately meanders around in a circle.

'Fuck, bastard fuck!' Yannis yells above the fumes. 'The port side prop is not working, it's fucking caught on something!'

'I'll go,' volunteers Bret, immediately fitting some goggles. 'Is it port left or right?'

'Left!' Yannis shouts.

Bret dives over the side and returns after a few exploratory oxygen-free dives with Saffron's mangled string tied thong.

'Can I keep this pal?' He asks Kevin, holding the thong up.

'Sure bud, but best ask Saffy. You know she's got a shit load more at the villa, come back and have a look. We also have a fridge rammed with booze.'

Saffy just giggles.'Be my guest, Bret.'

25
The Port and the Pharmacy

With the prop sorted, the group gets back to the harbour and all passengers pour off. The tip basket is empty apart from Anthony's offering: a bad poem about dolphins, and five thousand drachmas. The guests depart, as does Yannis, to have some kind of raki seizure. Saffron, like the Queen of Sheba, guides Kevin and Bret, who seem to be getting on famously, to the nearest bar next to the newspaper and cigarette kiosk. They find a table with a view of the harbour whilst Saffron scans the magazines in the kiosk and the glass phallic figurines filled with ouzo. Denholm chuckles at Margaritte, who looks over, disgusted. Allen attempts to rouse Anthony and Christian when Denholm walks over.

'Thanks man', he whispers, 'haven't had such a good time in years. Watercolours are fine but there's nothing like a bit of real cock and peachy girly ass.' He departs promptly before Allen can reply, in their Fantasy Hire car, leaving him and Penne to drag Christian and Anthony off the boat.

Allen wakes Anthony and drops him and the half-conscious Christian safely back from the waterfront. He chooses one of the white iron seafront chairs, one of the old antiquities resting in circular fashion around the partially—and equally old—white-painted olive trees. It is a fine place where the good old boys would usually sit with their half-true stories and worry beads.

'May we borrow your chair for ten minutes or so?' Allen asks.

'By all means, dear boy, locate me onto the bench here with Christian and we will support each other. I assume you want the chair to wheel Her Majesty to the pharmacy?'

'You got it,' says Allen.

Christian flops like an oversized rag doll on the bench. He stirs momentarily and mutters, 'beautiful dolphins, never realised they were so pink', before slipping back into a deep sleep. Anthony chuckles. 'Remember the brakes are knackered.'

Penne walks beside Allen, who pushes the chair back to the boat where Grace is sitting, rubbing her backside, an awkward thing to do from a prone position. 'If you think I'm going to the pharmacy in that bleeding thing you got another fink coming.'

Allen, who has frankly had enough of her nonsense and just wants to get back to the apartment to shag his betrothed, loses it. 'Shut the fuck up and get in!'

For once, Grace says nothing and sits quietly in the chair.

'These bleedin' cobbles we're going over ain't half hurting mi bum. Christ knows why they don't just tarmac the lot. I bet Christian's got contacts here who would get it done in an hour or two.'

Penne and Allen ignore her as they navigate the chair into the store. The pharmacist, a Greek woman in her late forties with dark black hair tied up in a bun, with a fine bone structure, looks concerned when she sees the chair, and even more so when she recognises Grace sitting in it. She has a small silver Orthodox crucifix around her slender neck, which she grasps desperately in one hand as she nervously backs away. Grace has obviously been a regular visitor since she has been on the island. She probably already has a loyalty card, but judging by the pharmacist's reaction, she certainly is not the mystery shopper.

'I've been bit on my ass by sommat. These muppets think I need the chair and some oxy acetylene.'

'No, no, no, madam. You have to go to the harbour for that, this is a chemist.'

'Wot I need the harbour to sort out my ass. We've just come from there and I ain't going back in this bleedin' chair.'

'What she really means is antihistamine.' Penne clarifies, calming the situation in fast flowing Greek. 'This woman is no friend of ours and is in fact a complete and utter prat.'

Back at the seafront bar, aptly named Janus Cocktails, Saffy returns from the souvenir kiosk with a full sleeve of Camel cigarettes, two ouzo-filled bottles embellished with a very largely-endowed erect phallus, and a small illustrated book published in Crete titled *Sex in Ancient Greece*. The first picture makes Saffy feel slightly flushed: two extremely well-hung blokes, one receiving oral from a sublime beautiful woman whilst she receives a sound pounding in the lower region, with the actual location unclear from the illustration. The vendor, Tobias, kindly puts everything in a white plastic bag but, seeing that the contents remain visible, double bags it for good measure. Saffy makes her way back to the bar where Kevin and Bret are engaged in deep conversation, probably about sport, or hot babes, or sport with hot babes.

'Hello boys.' She kisses Kevin on the cheek. 'I certainly hope you got me a drink because I've bought you both some prizes for your bravery on the boat trip today. Mainly for rescuing a poor maiden in clear distress and for being very entertaining.'

Both men stand up as she, Aphrodite, approaches the table. It is covered with a paper tablecloth with a printed image of the island in blue. Some fresh crusty bread and olives in a plate accommodate the centre. 'Fantastic to observe good male manners. Manners maketh man,' she claims, some twenty years too early, as she sits on a white plastic Janus Bar chair and reaches for a wooden cocktail stick for the olives.

'I assume this is mine?' Saffy picks up a rather large highball glass filled with Champagne and Cassis. 'Wrong glass though, boys, for a Kir Royale, but it's still very pleasant.' She eyes them both closely. 'I trust you naughty men haven't spiked this because I don't need spiking. You will, and I seriously mean *will*, do as you are told.'

'Yes, ma'am!' Bret and Kevin say in unison.

'Want some nuts?' Kevin asks, pointing to the table.

'You bet ya!' And after a suitable pause, she adds, 'Page three of this little book is rather interesting.'

'We ordered some fried calamari,' Brett adds, slightly nervously.

'Yummy, I like a good squid ring or two,' she teases, raising a Cleopatra plucked eyebrow.

'Best get these prats in a taxi and back to their villas.' Allen whispers. 'I have another surprise for you.'

They pick up Christian, leave the poet back in his chair and carry Grace, who is still complaining about her antihistamine cream, all the way to the taxi.

'We still going to the Owacle the day after tomorrow?'

Allen hesitates before replying. 'Haven't you had enough trips, Mrs Houseman? Why not see how your injury heals and let me know in the morning?'

'I already spoke to Yannis. He said it's on, so fuck off!' With that she slams the taxi door shut as gracefully as Grace can manage, trapping the plastic bag with the medication in the door.

'Four down, if you count the Crawfords, and one poet to go. Sounds like a bloody takeaway, doesn't it? It appears they don't need any help, judging by the laughter and the obvious body language.' Allen shrugs a shoulder in Kevin's, Bret's and Saffron's direction. Saffy waves.

'Have you seen those ouzo erectus cock bottles, Penne?'

'The whole port has seen them, I think!' She smiles. 'They are young, they are free, a bit like you and me. Well, mostly me, sex doll!'

'You sound like the poet now, *fiancée*,' smiles Allen. 'Oh, and thanks for the big up age check!'

After a quick call, Nikos agrees to take Anthony home in the company van, leaving Allen and Penne alone for once.

'Right! A drink first and then we have some serious business to attend to, involving warm water, the kitchen table and a pack of Bics, and I'm not talking Ritz here, but maybe Digestives after.' Allen asserts. 'Sounds good to you?'

'Do we need the squirty cream?' Asks Penne, raising an equally Cleopatra groomed eyebrow.

26
Plumbing

The anomalies of Greek plumbing have already been discussed, but it really does beg the question how these gods actually built the Parthenon in the fifth century, that classical triumph of civil engineering. Allen has other plumbing issues to hand, however, more external fascia like the nicked Elgin Marbles rather than actual excrements.

Penne mounts the old pine kitchen table on all fours, waiting naked, listening to Van Morrison playing. Allen puts the hot, lavender-scented water in a stainless-steel bowl bought at the Conran Store back in the UK directly below Penne's glorious backside. She rests her head on the pristine cotton pillows Allen has positioned for her when he covered the table with white towels. The aromatherapy candles he has purchased on a previous Athenian trip are lit, and the Bics and Dove soap are prepped and ready to go. A full Brazilian waxing done this way is both highly enjoyable but does require skill, a steady hand, and certainly no mobile phone interruption. Allen is halfway through a perfectly shaven bush when the phone rings. It is the Devil. Again.

'Alleeeen,' screeches the wild voice on the end of the phone, which is now covered with soap and pubic hair. 'There's shit in our bedroom and it fuckin stinks!'

Shit usually does, considers Allen idly whilst surveying Penne's truly fantastic vaginal work like any true artist would. 'I'll Send Nikos and the maid over, Mrs Houseman, sleep in the other bedroom and open the windows.' He ends the call and chucks the phone in the sink, which fortunately only contains used moist bath towels to cushion the landing.

'Is it squirty cream time now, or do you need to get the sewer rods out?' She asks.

'The only rod I'm getting out is this baby.' Allen confirms by unzipping his shorts. 'But yes, I'll get the cream. Would you like some chocolate chip too? Or maybe a 99?'

'Stick with a 69 and don't get Mr Softy.'

'Coming right up!'

'But not too soon please, sex doll!' She purrs.

Nikos calls early the next morning. Allen's phone buzzes from the sink. He slips on the remains of the now sour squirty cream in his attempt to reach it.

'I'm going to bed now, you bastard. However, I want more money, so does the maid, and we both would like a life. We spent all night cleaning up after that cow, simply because she's been putting her ass wipe tissues down the sodding toilet and not in the bin beside it. You know, the bin with the sign, in red, stating use THIS, and NOT the toilet, for any sanitary products!'

Allen barely listens to Nikos's tirade, adding at a convenient break, 'Sorry buddy. I think I've dislocated my hip, I've just slipped on the tiles.'

'Oh fuck off!' Yells Nikos, terminating the call.

27
Ditch the fish

Allen's archaeological aspirations and artistically underrated accomplishments have always fascinated, and filled, Penne with admiration since the first time they met at that cheap hotel in Omonia Square in Athens.

The square would have benefitted from being sprayed with a load of ammonia to disinfect the place. Detritus, from the sad drug users, thrived along with pimps and pick pockets and con men. A little like mid-eighteenth century London, maybe William Hogarth, and Gin Lane as a comparison, but without the syringes. The hotel was optimistically named the Apollo Amore. The love theme was vaguely accurate, but in view of NASA and Greek mythology connection, it was completely wrong. It was basically a huge brothel with a piano bar, no pimps and pole dancing, but it had flexible check-in times and billing arrangements.

Allen was there for the large Yamaha grand piano. Halfway through his set that day, playing the unsuitable Hotel California, he made eye contact with Penne.

'Christ, she's bloody gorgeous!' He mumbled to himself.

The punter she was with looked Japanese and was at least six inches shorter than her. Penne looked worse than bored. There was little conversation happening and the pathetic prospect of some sushi to look forward to upstairs. Allen had never really liked cold meat, and judging by Penne's body language, neither did she. This guy looked like a piece of raw tuna without the fin. After Allen's interpretation of the awesome Brian Ferry's "Slave to Love", the Tuna left for the toilets, presenting an opportunity for Allen, who went straight in with a pickup line and a rather scruffy business card.

'Hello, beautiful person, this is my card, ditch the fish, the next song is for you.'

'Who's the fish?' Penne shouts as Allen makes a quick exit back to the stage and piano. *Trout mouth, Mr Whitebait, Tenpole Tudor*, Allen wanted to say.

'The fucker sitting next to you,' Allen points to the half-consumed Blue Hawaiian with a pink umbrella.

He promptly started playing "You're the Best Thing" by The Style Council, changing the lyrics slightly from "you're the best that ever happened" to "that could ever happen", looking directly at her. She seemed to know the words and to have noticed the change. She thought about it whilst looking at the business card as the Tuna resumed his sweaty seat next to her.

Allen had four other songs in his set to go through, and he really didn't expect or want any encore. He just hoped to be paid. The last song should have again been "Surfing USA" , a rather inappropriate tune for the venue, but Allen decided to play Mink DeVille's "Spanish Stroll" instead.

He paused directly before the Tuna, leaving the piano to pick up the guitar and sing.

'"With a finger on your eyebrow and left hand on your hip, you're such a lady killer, you think your so slick".' He looked directly at Mr Snapper, his white twelve-string guitar now musically on fire, fret facing forward like an AK 47 and pointing in the Trout's direction. The Fish chucked some cash on the table and left. Penne looked impressed.

'You owe me money.' She said.

'And you owe me fish-free fingers,' he added, sitting down in the Tuna's seat next to her, to muted applause. 'Wanna get out of this dump?'

'I'm meant to be working.'

'This ain't working, hon,' Allen pointed around. 'This is slavery, with possible infection and probable chains. You got a pimp?'

'No, I'm self-employed but cheating on my tax returns. I choose my own marks.'

'I take it you dig seafood then?'

Penne laughed. 'Let's get out of here. There's a place, a nice place, I know.'

'I'll get my guitar case and mikes, maybe someone will think I'm Antonio Banderas and pay me.'

28
Ragonesi's Maltese pizzeria

They found a booth indoors with a view of Athens, the pinnacle being the floodlights on the Acropolis high up in the distance. They ordered what Penne suggested, two calzone filled with salami, ham, mozzarella, Pecorino, capers, and eggs, complimented with a jug of the local red wine, bread, and Greek black olives. Penne knew the proprietor, so the food and service, even at this late hour, were excellent.

The conversation was good, fast-flowing, and flirty. Ragonesi was an elderly, grey-haired, Moses-looking man, with facial hair that seemed to sprout in every direction. He had the bluest of blue eyes that still held their youth, and a golden hoop in one ear. His hands were large, yet stubby, and calloused from years of manual work. He wore a tee-shirt with a red heart and an "I" above it and "Athens" underneath. His blue-and-white striped trousers, a sort of ex-military or ex-prison look, paired painfully with Greek leather sandals. He embraced Penne like a daughter and eyed up Allen with both suspicion and hatred in the eyes.

'This guy is okay, he is no punter, just a friend.' Penne informed him. Ragonesi's mood instantly softened, and a broad grin appeared on his lips.

'Save this beauty, young man, do it now. I know her from a child, she 's a good girl.' Ragonesi's speech came out in broken English.

It had been ages since anyone had called Allen "young" so he stood, drink in hand, and raised his glass to the *maître*. '*Yamas kyrios*, I will do my best.'

'The best you do must be the very best, my Brit friend, to save Penne from all this,' he gestures outside with stubby fingers. 'She dances, did you know?'

'Yeah I dance,' confirms Penelope, 'but not in titty bars. I do classical ballet at Maria Pothitou School of Dance in the city. It is my dream, my passion, my life, but maybe a fool's dream.' She takes a large sip of wine and toys with a couple of olives.

'It's only a fool and their money that can be separated, not a fool and their dream, or their dance,' says Allen. 'Better to do the *Nutcracker* in a pirouette on stage than in bed with Johnny out of his depth.'

'You know, for an English you are quite the philosopher,' laughs Penne. 'A strange find.'

'We do have some, philosophers I mean. But they mainly live on the south coast somewhere past Hove and towards Chichester.'

'These places I do not know, Allen, maybe you show me one day?'

'No, hon. You stick with Greece and its glorious islands, this is all the culture anyone could ask for and you've got it made.'

She lights a cigarette and lets the smoke twist and swirl upwards in an ever-changing mood. Allen realises they like each other.

'Why are you hiding behind that menu?' She asks him. 'You've peered over the top of it for the last ten minutes, do you not like the food? The calzone here is great and my company can't be that bad!'

'I know, I'm just getting a bit hot that's all.'

'Why do you get so hot, Allen? Is it because of that chick over there?' Penne points towards the window to the pavement opposite. There is a lady looking in from behind the restaurant glass. 'She watches you, Allen. She is lovely, isn't she?'

'I know that already,' answers Allen, 'however, I need to tell you something. I know that girl ain't a girl, and just for one night only, one night only, I did sleep with him … her! It was all a big mistake. Fun, I admit, but a one-time thing. But, hon, you need to know, I didn't at the time, you understand? I didn't think he had an eight-inch cock below the thong, girly top and hold-ups, and I needed company.'

'Oh! Forget it, Allen, it's okay! He's a cousin of mine and this is Greece, so no worries. Did you enjoy it? Penne smiles.

'It was interesting, but not something I would wish to pursue,' replies Allen.

'Good! You can come home with me then, my big sex doll! Maybe we make plans one day.'

29
Home time

After World War two had come to its eventual close and the Germans, Italians and allied forces had ceased their destructive activities, a calm returned to Athens until the third stage of the Greek Civil War a few months later. Hostilities on top of more hostilities, this time Greek on Greek. On one side stood the British, Americans and the Greeks, and on the other, Yugoslavia, Albania, Bulgaria, and the Greeks. It was, politically-speaking, one huge mess.

Penne's home consists of a one-bedroom flat constructed within an area that hosted much of the civil war and destruction during those long, troubled times. The municipality of Omonoia, another post-modernist, partially rebuilt civic dream, emerged. A world of drugs, vice, violence, and, strangely, good hotels. During daylight hours, the place heaves and beats normally like many other areas in many other cities. At night, however, it assumes the mantel of Gotham City without Batman. Not quite as energetic or futuristic as *Blade Runner* with the glorious Rutger Hauer, but with neon signs and wailing sirens.

Penne closes her steel-lined door and locks the three bolts.

'I take it you don't want me to go?' Allen watches the third bolt lock securely.

'That quite depends on whether you are a good boy or not. But no, the locks are to keep the world out, not you in.' She moves away from the door to the kitchen. 'What would you like to drink? I don't have much, I'm afraid, but I've got vodka somewhere.'

'You know, I was going to suggest vodka. Do you have ice?'

'This is Athens, not Moscow, and with no air conditioning. Ice is as essential to keep things cool. Like vodka is in Moscow to survive their bad weather.'

'Fair point.' Says Allen.

After a lot of extraordinary sex, Allen wonders if he actually had a bell end left, but basks in his post-sex bliss before speaking. That, and him needing to catch his breath after giving Penne her third oral orgasm of the evening.

'We have to clarify certain ground rules here, and it's all a bit complex. Very English, and a dilemma which could either go right or horribly wrong, so diplomacy is needed.'

'Can you use your tongue again? And it doesn't mean for talking.'

'Hon, I don't believe you are listening to a word I'm saying here, are you?'

'Yes,' she replies fiddling with Allen's left nipple, 'but now is not the time for talking, Allen, now is the time for loving and tomorrow is the time for talking.'

'So that being the case, can I take you out for dinner tomorrow to say thank you as I'd love to get to know you better? Quite how getting to know you further is possible considering my love-making has been everywhere on your gorgeous body.'

'I don't know.'

'I can afford dinner tomorrow but can't afford tonight's', teases Allen.

'Bravo,' claps Penne. 'You are the diplomat! It's a good job I'm broad-minded. And yes, I would be delighted. I like you, you silly Englishman.'

That sheer chance encounter is how they both met. An unusual circumstance at an unusual time and an unusual relationship was formed, with no further mention of Cora Evangeline Roma.

30
The Royal Marines

'We need a submersible cage.'

'What, like a Gimp thing? Allen asks.

'And a winch thing.'

'Where exactly do you think this is, Alise, the Exton Commando Training Centre in Devon?'

'No, but well done for your geographical skills. Have you, by any chance, signed the official secrets act or do I need to pop around and kill you?'

After a suitable pause, Allen chooses not to respond.

'How big a cage do you need? Are we talking for sharks here or can I get something adapted?'

'Think of four lobster pots lashed together on a good length of wire rope.'

'We can do that,' says Allen.

'Or a couple of metal supermarket trolleys we get back home welded together,' adds Finn from somewhere in the background.

'Okay fellas. I'll talk to Yannis later, he welds and knowns a shit load about winches and boat crap. However, please don't come round and kill me because I've just got engaged, so get to the Windy Bar this afternoon and I'll have some answers for you. Just don't bring guns, knives, or any fucking kung fu.' Alistair laughs.

Penne returns from the only seafront tourist shop clutching a carrier bag to find Allen sitting on the low stone harbour wall, deep in thoughts.

'What's the matter with you, Spider Brain?' She looks at him with concern. 'You look troubled.'

'Nothing, peaches, just thinking about the marines, that's all. What's in the bag?'

Penne throws it at him and he catches it with ease. 'Open it,' she smiles.

Allen pulls out a large black tee-shirt with the words "You the man" emblazoned in white print on its front. 'Aw, hon, I love it! Maybe more apt for a marine though!'

'You're the only diver I need.'

Allen gives her a kiss. 'Fancy the Windy Bar for some lunch, girlfriend?'

'Fiancée,' she corrects him, throwing a look at her sparkling finger.

'Fancy the Windy Bar for some lunch, if we can still move that is, *fiancée*?'

'Mmm, that would be lovely. That Grace cow will not be present, I take it?'

'No, just you, me, the marines, and the poet no doubt.'

'No beanie hats either?'

'No, and no Nikos because he's still pissed with me about the Houseman's toilet problem.'

'Fine then, baby. It sounds good to me.'

The Meltemi winds were throwing a strong, dry northern wind rippling the Windy Bar's awning and rattling its restraining wire hawsers against the chrome stanchions supporting the white sail-like cover. The noise it makes is not unpleasant, some find it relaxing even, unlike Allen's phone which suddenly rings.

'Where's Christian? Can't he help you with whatever it is you're calling me about?' Allen asks her tiredly.

'He's shut himself inside the living room watching some Greek TV adverts about saucepans.'

'And does this interest him?' Allen thinks he sounds like a psychiatrist.

'Our own kitchen is taken over by chickens.'

'Maybe he should catch one and rustle up a quick *coq au vin* in one of those pans!'

'Cock of what? Alleeen! One of the bastard's just attacked me!'

'What with? A rolling pin or the set of stainless-steel cooking knives? Look, just get the broom and shoo them out! Then take the broom to Christian and tell him to stick it. You know what I mean.' Allen ends the call as Finn and Alise approach, both wearing Docs.

Mateo has the freshly-welded gimp cage with a winch and a huge roll of wire cable that Yannis has dropped off earlier, along with an extortionate bill. There is a note that says "Cash only". Yannis has done a fine job though, and sure enough, two metal supermarket trolleys are welded together side by side. The wheels were ground off and the push handles sheared off and re-welded together across the centre of the two trolleys. It looked a bit like an oversized trug or a sledge without its runners. There is even a cleat to attach the wire hawser. Finn walks under the awning, humming 'These Boots Are Made for Walkin". He catches the poet admiring his boots.

'A fine song by a fine star,' confirms Anthony. 'Wrote a poem about stars, want to hear it?' It's called "Wish".

No one can really stop him. Allen wishes he would shut up for once so can enjoy his lunch. No.

Wish

I have caught the stars
to weave with silken light,
a garland for your hair.
And—

He is stopped short in his reading as Mateo's wretched goats escape their enclosure and storm inside the restaurant like the plague. For a starter, they remove, and consume, the paper tablecloths, what is left of Penne's eggplant moussaka and Allen's high-fat burger. The chime of goat bells is immense. The Thompsons immediately step into action, without their guns, knives, and kung fu accessories, military training at its best. With Allen's and Mateo's help, they effectively corner the goats behind the saloon doors that lead to a small open door into the restaurant kitchen at the back. On their way, the goats knock over a bottle of Tequila, which they start to lap before sampling the Galliano as a sort of chaser. Quite apt really, as the men chase the drunk goats.

'It's okay,' Mateo says, slamming shut the bar door and top. 'We are not busy, I will let them out through the back door from the kitchen. Just watch the hot fat boys. You'd think Nikos would help with this goat shit.'

'Just leave him,' shouts Allen, 'he's had far too much shit to sort these past few days. I'll check out the gate above the pool. Please just get us all a drink Mateo. You may need the AA for the pissed up goats, though. That big white sod seems to really have developed a taste for it.'

'Fuck the bastards!'

Readily marinated goat stifado, he thinks. He spots Alise examining the cage.

'That will do very well indeed,' he admires, 'very well indeed. Greek engineering at its best.'

'Have you seen the bill yet?' Allen cautions him.

'No worries bud, we're on expenses.'

'Can I ask what exactly it is for?' Penne inquires.

'No you may not, ma'am,' Finn and Alice claim in unison. 'But good job Allen.'

Finn gives him a high five. 'We, marines, never forget, you know.'

Forget what, thinks Allen.

'Well, pissed goats and gimp cages, let's just hope the poet has forgotten his poem.'

Which of course, as any poet knows, he has not.

'Not now, Anthony, dear friend, it's not the right time.' He looks at the poet doing some breathing exercises to limber up. 'Let's all just relax, have some fries, and drink this cold wine in lovely peace and quiet. Maybe listen to the wind ruffling the awning or take in the distant tinkle of drunk goat bells, total peace and a view the gods have created.'

That is until Allen's mobile rings again.

'We fucked off the chickens!' Grace shouts.

'Great work, we fucked off the goats.'

'You fucked some goats?'

'No, no, certainly not!' He replies, briefly explaining the great escape, without the great Donald Pleasence.

'Okay, enough about that crap, Alleeen. Wot I want to know now, is the owacle trip still on for tomorrow?'

'I've seen and spoken to Yannis this morning. It's a long haul from here, you do realise, followed by a long taxi drive? It's in an air-conditioned Mercedes though, so you should be comfortable. Take plenty of drachmas for the entrance fee and tips.'

'We don't tip.'

'Lunch is thrown in,' he continues, 'and you depart from the port here at seven am. Yannis knows you both and will be there, with the big boat, the Boreas.'

'Are you going with us?'

'No, it's just you, Mr Houseman and Yannis, so all very intimate. You should be back around nine in the evening, but the boat is very comfortable, with berths if you fancy a nap.'

'Who do you think we are, Alleen? A couple of fucking pensioners like the Cwarfods?' Grace answers with her usual politeness.

'I trust you have a fine day, Mrs Houseman-Smith, and that the Oracle tells you all that you need to know.' Allen puts the phone down and sighs.

Penne looks at her ring and whispers. 'Is it always like this? Poets, drunk rampaging goats, marines, drunk rampaging tourists? My job's a quiet life by comparison, at least I only have to deal with one nut case at a time.'

'No, hon, not always and not forever, I promise.' Allen turns his phone off and contemplates a change in career might be in order.

31
An interesting arrangement

According to Mateo, Bret the First Aider and Gardener from south Derbyshire has moved into Saffy and Kevin's villa. Allen has referred to his Laskarina training manual for useful tips on how to accommodate a *ménage à trois* but the tour operator's volume seems to have sadly neglected this proposition. However, judging by body language, all three seem to be having a fantastic holiday at the Villa Hibiscus. Saffy appears to be completely in charge of all the decision-making, but not in a hard dominatrix sort of way, and the boys, arms linked shoulder-to-shoulder, look like they have known each other for years. Allen wonders what Saffy's and Kevin's relationship is exactly like, back home in the UK.

The three appear to be heading for the most hedonistic bar on the island, Janus Cocktails, the home to the famous Anus cocktail. They have purchased a huge pink inflatable pool armchair. In reality, the "throuple" needs a sofa to accommodate three, and maybe some inflatable foot stools. Allen watches them sit at the best table under the equally pink awning umbrellas. Saffy notices Penne and Allen by the harbour wall and frantically waves them over.

Christ, thinks Allen, *my orgy days are well and truly over, and I'm newly engaged to a part-time escort.* He looks at Penne for consent.

'This might be entertaining. Come on, we should join them!'

'Okay, hon, but I'm not sharing you with anyone else.'

'Oh, Allen you are so sweet! But stop worrying, this is Greece after all!'

'Yeah… but they are all Brits, and I know Brits. On holiday and at home, and they ain't all like Prince Charles or Peter Kay.'

'Well, sex doll, I certainly ain't for sale anymore.' She holds out her hand to Allen, which he takes, and starts guiding him towards the young tourists. 'In fact,' she looks down at her ring, 'I need a career change.'

'Shall we order then, boys and girls? Because considering what you've told me about your interrupted lunch earlier with Mateo's drunk goats, you must be hungry?'

Bret signals the waitress and orders in superb Greek. The waitress looks down at her pad after his triumph and says, 'Is that Greek? Sorry love, but I'm from Bolton. I can do a little Italian.' Her cheeks redden. 'I don't actually mean do a short Italian! Although I probably could or maybe even have…' She goes redder and shakes her pretty head. 'English is probably the best.'

'Calamari then please.' Penne observes her obvious confusion.

'It's squid.'

'Oh, and how would you like that done?'

'Cooked. In a light batter.' Bret smiles. 'You normally only say that for red meat.'

'Sorry,' replies the waitress. 'I'm a bit out of my comfort zone here, I'm new.'

'No worries,' says Allen, as the others consider what to order. The waitress departs and returns with the usual crusty bread, condiments, and a jug of wine.

'You all seem to be getting on well?' Penne observes with no subtlety and very tongue in cheek.

'The boys here are my bodyguards. It's a strange land full of danger for a vulnerable girl,' comments Saffy, raising an eyebrow.

The evening turns out to be a riotous success, many laughs, far too much wine and innuendos aplenty. Further momentum is added when the Meltemi wind kicks in. A sudden severe gust kicks up and blows the pink inflatable armchair off. It hovers strangely like a small UFO before deciding to join an adjacent table of four rather bored-looking Germans and two young kids. The kids find the interruption highly amusing when the chair demolishes papa's lasagne and then moves off up the strip in front of the bar, nearly knocking an elderly Greek man off his Mego three-wheeler moped. The chair and one pink umbrella end up over the low harbour wall and in the water, born idly towards mainland Greece. If it hadn't been for Kevin and Bret's joint intervention, the things might have reached Athens by the morning.

'See what I mean?' Saffy comments to Penne. 'Two guys are

often better than one, especially when they're drenched in sea water.' Penne giggles. 'Oh and Allen, good idea to get the bill. Maybe buy the Germans a drink? Don't worry about their lasagne, the Greeks can't make it and I don't think Dad was enjoying it anyway. The cats seem to like it enough, particularly that one with the big orange ears, look at him go!'

'We'll split the bill.'

32
Delphi

The Oracle occupies a site on the south-western slope of Mount Parnassus, overlooking the coastal plain to the south and the valley of Phocis. The archaeological site is a UNESCO world heritage protectorate and is recognised as having had a great influence in the ancient world. Evidence excavated, and that which remained intact, indicates that it was built by the most civic-minded Greek states for the purpose of a lasting demonstration of fundamental Hellenic unity. Delphi grew rich as the seat of Pythia, the high priestess known as the Oracle, high most of the time on drugs and various supposedly underground vapours. She was consulted about important decisions throughout the ancient classical world. The Ancient Greeks considered the centre of the world to be in Delphi, marked by the stone monument known as the Omphalos, the belly button of all civilisation. Another good reason for Grace not to visit. The Greek history of the Oracle is a tale of gods, priests and priestesses, guardians, invaders, drugs, and superstition. The Omphalos was discovered when Zeus released his great eagles from each end of his decreed world, which crossed in the sky above Delphi. From this point on, Zeus had hurled a vast stone from the heavens to mark the spot which remained in place until it was excavated and placed under cover at the museum on site. Its landing spot is still marked by a large cone-shaped stone set on a low square plinth. Superstition decrees that the Oracle, within the Temple of Apollo, may still be questioned by anyone who chooses to, but only in the summer months. It is said to enlighten those who wish to fully know their destiny or future.

It is seven in the morning the following day, and the sea is flat and becalmed. Grace and Christian arrive on time and greet Yannis, who fires up the engine on the mighty twin prop white Boreas. Grace is unsuitably dressed, as usual, in an overly-tight red tube which shows off her gold daisy belly-button piercing. The act is somewhat disrespectful since the Omphalos stone is considered to be the navel of the world. She has covered her legs, though, and totters in ridiculous white heels. Christian is wearing a highly-fashionable shell suit covered with logos and clashing colours, an image far too young for him, and complemented with white socks and Adidas trainers. He is smoking a cigar, as usual. He hands Yannis a large wad of money.

'That should cover all,' he says between two bronchial coughs, the residue from which he spits over the side of the boat.

'Nice.' Yannis says. He finishes counting the notes. He has been overpaid. He makes sure to work out Allen's cut and starts up the boat.

Allen's cellphone rings. The Devil again. Surely, it is far too early for things to have gone wrong yet. He reaches over Penne to retrieve his mobile from under the bedside table and accidentally wakes her up in the process.

'Hello,' he answers, summoning up extreme friendliness.

'We're on the fucking boat Alleeeeeen and off to the Owacle!'

'Thanks for letting me know at this early hour, Mrs Houseman,' he grunts, whilst gently massaging Penne's right nipple. 'I trust it will tell you all you need to know about your future. Just please don't get into trouble again.' Allen knows this is a fairly fatuous thing to say to Grace.

'As if, fucker,' she replies unconvincingly.

33
The journey

Yannis and his caterers have really made Grace and Christian proud, with a platter of cold snacks including prawn cocktails, vol-au-vents with various fillings, cocktail sausages on sticks with Greek feta, and other hors d'oeuvres, all washed down with a copious amount of Amyntas Blanc de Noir, a pleasant Greek sparkling wine. Lunch on board the Boreas, with its walnut interior, is truly fantastic. Christian and Grace even look happy together for once, and the wine helps disguise the boat's slight smell of fuel.

Yannis navigates the Boreas through the Gulf of Corinth, following the ancient route of many travellers from the eighth century BCE who wished to consult the Oracle. Their eventual destination is the port of Itea, which is two kilometres west of Kirra, where the ancients would have originally landed. A taxi ride in a black air-conditioned Mercedes is booked to take the modern travellers from the contemporary world to the archaeological site. It is roughly ten miles up Mount Parnassus prior to reaching the rising ground of the terrain. Yannis cannot wait. The tour is nearly halfway over, and nothing has gone wrong yet.

He moors the boat. Sure enough, his cousin Socrates is waiting in the black chartered car. Yannis prays and signs his chest in relief. Soc is not the most reliable fellow in town and is prone to a drink or two before work. Today, however, he looks sober and in full control of himself. He knows the plan: take the Brits to Delphi, show them the Oracle, the temples and museums, then bring the Brits back to the boat safely.

Cousin Socrates is of medium height, but overweight, a possible consequence of both overeating and being seated all day, driving for a living. His hair is short, black, and straight, with no hint of grey, although Yannis firmly believes he dyes it as his goatee is completely grey. He has the look of an inverted badger with black hooded eyes and far too many worry lines for a man in his mid-forties. He wears silver mirrored Ray-Ban aviator sunglasses and a black, loose-fitting cotton suit to match the car. He looks like one of the bad guys out of *The Rockford Files* or *Magnum P.I.* but he is realistically a very pleasant and polite man.

He holds the rear door open for Grace first. A burst of cool air greets her. 'Mmm' she purrs as she gets in. Soc quickly walks to the other side for Christian.

'No smoking in here, please sir, extinguish your cigar,' he orders politely. Christian, for once, resists the argument, probably pleased to have some cool air.

Socrates is even wearing his best black Denton peaked cap, only normally reserved for celebrities like Sigourney Weaver, the goddess he has had the honour to drive to the same destination, and Demi Moore.

'How fine are these wheels!' Grace admires, loudly belching. 'Sorry, far too many hors d' oeuvres.'

Yannis observes the introduction and waves sympathetically at his cousin with a raised eyebrow. Socrates promptly takes his cap off.

'Naww leave your bleedin' hat on,' shouts Grace from the back of the car.

Yannis pays Soc, who looks relieved. Socrates puts his hat back on.

'Time the trip, Socrates, as we have a long way to return to Kea, and try to steer the visitors away from trouble. Christian's okay but his wife inhabits another planet, and it certainly isn't ours.'

'Will do,' confirms Soc. 'The boat smells of exhaust fumes, by the way.'

'I know, cousin, I'm going to check that whilst you're taking our guests away.'

'Good luck with that!' Soc glances at the Boreas, then gets into the driver's seat, knocking his capped head on the small crucifix and St Christopher in the process, which fall from the rear-view mirror. Grunting in Greek, he reaches for the passenger foot well to retrieve the Saint and the crucifix. He might need them.

34
The Oracle

All that remains nowadays of the great Temple of Apollo are six broken Doric columns surmounted by a capital and assorted excavated masonry. The centre, or belly button of the world, is marked by a large stone cone on a square plinth surrounded by a low rusty iron rail to stop tourists from getting too close.

'The Temple had, or has,' he can't remember as he reels out his limited Delphi history tour guide spiel, 'a carved Greek inscription which read "Know Thyself".'

He hopes Mrs Houseman-Smith takes this on board as he pulls into the strangely empty designated parking area. It is one in the afternoon, and siesta time beckons. This doesn't stop the UNESCO guides from doing their duty as they gesture the car into a space further away from the admission and ticket office.

'There's fucking loads of pillars, rocks and shit!' Grace observes like a true historian. 'It's a shame they're all broken and fallen over. You'd think they would repair the fuckers a bit.' She mutters, getting out of the air-conditioned car and into the blazing heat of another day in scorching paradise. 'Christian!' She shouts, 'Look, they got pillars here like ours at home outside the front door, but ours are new!'

Soc wanders off to get the tickets, shaking his head whilst Grace waves over to an attendant who looks scared.

'Where's the bloody owacle? I got some questions for it.' The parking attendant signals in the vague direction of the Temple of Apollo.

She attempts to slip on her white heels on the unfinished, uneven ground, but ends up twisting her ankle. 'Bastard! That hurt! They need you here, Christian, with your road surfacing stuff.'

Christian ignores her and lights another cigar. The smoke gently curls upwards and mixes with the sweet cypress air and the pure blue sky. There is not a cloud in sight. He moves off to one of the benches to sit and take in the view of the ancient city. It is the perfect spot for a few holiday guest apartments, maybe a quad track too. His mind wanders to a potential business project and the possibility of purchasing some of this carved rock for artificial ponds back in the UK.

'You comin?' Grace calls him in her best falsetto screech as Soc returns with the tickets, beautifully printed with Delphi pictures.

'Naw, I'll stay here, thanks.' He shouts. 'Take in the view, frankly it's all just rock and rubble or rock and roll.' It is a poor joke, but then it is Christian.

'Suit yourself, you old miserable bastard!'

She heads off up the path to the Temple of Apollo and the belly button of the world. *Shame the umbilical cord ain't still attached,* thinks Christian, *it might strangle her. Still, there is always the possibility of a snake bite, or her finding the Medusa. Perhaps she'll gaze into her eyes and get turned into another slab of all this knackered stone lying around.* He mind wonders to his business idea and state-of-the-art water features.

Why this visit to the Oracle is so important to Grace, no one apart from Allen will ever know. At home, Grace is strangely superstitious. She will never walk under ladders, will never put any of her vast collection of shoes on a table and, most definitely, will never have a peacock feather in the house. She also has a sort of mixed religious shrine with candles, crystals, incense and the odd Buddha statue in a recessed oval alcove, specifically designed for the lounge, next to the log burner. The varied religious iconography, not a devotion to any specific faith, is so she can cover all eventualities.

Allen is overseeing the departure and arrival of other guests. Supervision tasks are easy, with the newcomers all staying at the same hotel, the Kea Plaza. It is a perfect and completely uncomplicated process, merely an exchange at reception and a promise of a tour talk in the following few days. The Plaza is a small and intimate family-run hotel with donkeys for the kids to ride on the beach. Only the undernourished ones, of course. The kids, not the poor donkeys. Some animal defenders had complained, even though someone else, an anti-animal hater, had pointed out that Jesus rode one. Amusingly, another equally-interested equestrian had added, 'Well, he was only a skinny cunt and not a fat bastard.' Quite another fantastically successful civic meeting.

The leavers merely needed assistance boarding the ferry with their luggage. There were goodbye hugs and tears, with sincere promises to be back the following year, which they won't hold, and assurances that they will stay in touch, which they won't do either, unless they are the crazy painters, but the Crawfords have another week to run their car into the ground and create more ground—or car-breaking—artwork.

Allen's phone rings just as the eager new tourists have been left at their hotel and the leavers have departed on the Dolphin. By now, the new tourists are undoubtedly opening the complimentary hampers and trying not to wretch on the cold dolmades. Allen looks at his home screen. Guess who.

'Alleeeeen!' She screams in the speaker. 'A fucking Delphi guard has got me locked up next to the ticket office where some sweaty Greek thugs are planning shit. I'm sure they want sex with me!'

In your dreams. 'Where are they holding you?'

'In some pissing cupboard between the ticket office and the bogs. It bleedin' reeks in here.'

'What exactly have you done, Mrs Houseman Smith?'

'I only rubbed my tits on the navel of the world!' Grace says as if it were a normal thing to do. 'It's a spiritual thing! But some fascist saw me climb over the railings and do it.'

Fuck sake! Allen keeps up his composed calm. 'And why exactly would you want to rub your naked breasts on the Omphalos in the Greek countryside?'

'Because my tits are still slightly swollen, Allen. Put it together, man! Belly buttons, previous sickness, mother of the world stuff. I've lost two fucking babies, Allen, and I'm out of time, mi aviaries are fucked. I miscarried three months ago in the bath at home.'

Allen is in deep shock at this point, and really hurting for Grace, even though he still thinks she is a complaining trout. 'Does Christian know?'

'Course not,' sobs Grace. 'He only knows if one of his bleedin' cigars are missing, not his kids.'

Allen immediately takes charge, resisting the urge be sick.

'Sweet mother of God. That is truly awful,' he says rather weakly.

But then what can one really say when hearing such a sad revelation? 'Hold on, Mrs Houseman-Smith. I'll have you out of there in five minutes. Be calm, five minutes, okay?'

'Call me, Grace,' she sobs, 'you've earned it.'

Allen is straight on his mobile to Yannis who is immediately on his phone to Socrates, who has missed all the action because of a short nap caused by a quick swig of Brandy, the aroma of which is disguised by a copious amount of minty chewing gums. Christian is nowhere to be seen, having wandered off with a newfound zeal for archaeology, quad bikes and water features. It is up to the mighty Soc to sort the mess out, and by all accounts he is up for a fight. He has even put on his black fingerless leather driving gloves to deal with the officers. Grace is released almost immediately when the site guards observe what appears to be the spectacled, gloved gangster-like man approaching and carrying a large spanner.

'Home. Now,' orders Socrates. 'No argument, please.'

Grace and Christian return to the back seat silently, within the air-conditioned safety of the Mercedes.

Grace adjusts her top for maximum modesty. 'Thank you to Soc.'

For once, she is truly genuine.

Soc nods. 'All part of the service, ma'am.'

35
Home is where the heart is

'Where'd you get to when I needed you?' Grace asks. 'I assume pissing around in the bushes with your sad dreams or someone else.'

'Little chance of both,' replies Christian after some thought. 'You've screwed up most of my dreams and Delphi certainly ain't my idea of clubland. There's no fucker on the site. I was actually taking a shit by the amphitheatre as the bogs down here fucking reek.'

'Huh, one thing we can agree on, then,' sulks Grace. 'And you can't smoke in here.'

'Fuck off, bitch,' he spits.

'Sod off, you, complete cunt.'

'Please, please, dear people, if you will not be good to each other, then just say nothing, this is what wise men do, they say nothing,' Socrates instructs them, living up to this philosophical name.

The remainder of the journey back to the boat happens in complete silence. Except for a brief stop for Grace to buy a huge watermelon from an aged road-side vendor sleeping below his parasol in a faded seventies deckchair. She drops the melon on her way back to the car and it shatters, bleeding pips, juice and pulp onto the sun-baked road. She thinks about ringing Allen but cries instead, trying to get the pips out of her white stilettos, which now have a broken heel. The vendor, slightly stuck in his chair, kindly brings her another one.

'Here, no charge.'

'There's always a price to pay for everything,' she sobs.

The old man does not understand but holds his palms out as a gesture of faith, hope or charity. He tries his best with the little English he knows. 'A hand of friendship or a fist of hate.'

The car pulls up at the big white Boreas, which looks as fine as ever in the harbour. Socrates hands over his guests to Yannis.

'Never again, cousin, never again.'

Yannis, by means of an apology, hands him over more cash. Socrates seems pleased, or at least compensated.

'I'll go and try to clean all this watermelon out the car now. You might want this,' he gives him Grace's stiletto heel, 'it's madame's.'

'Well, I didn't think it was yours or Mr Houseman's, not in white anyway.'

The sea gently laps the sides of the boat. A bird cries overhead and a young girl rides past on a bicycle that is far too big for her. It all looks very David Lynch in a Greek slow motion kind of way. Yannis notices the name on the side of the bike, it reads "Destiny".

The island of Kea becomes visible and closer by the second as the twin props of the Boreas power the sleek craft through the water. Its highest mountain, Profitis Ilias, a big, dormant volcanic rock pile which rises to 561 meters above sea level, protrudes modestly from the lower lying ground. It is covered with patches of green cypresses, olive, almond, and stunted oak trees. Elias, the Latin for Elijah, is known as a messenger of God according to the *Books of Kings* found in the Hebrew Bible and the Quran. He is reputed to be something of a miracle maker, able to raise the dead, set fire to the living, and bring forth fire from the sky. A bit like the Human Torch in comic books, without the Lycra suit. Fire, however, remains a key word.

It will never be conclusively established what exactly caused the explosion and the sinking of the mighty Boreas so close to home. There were two amazingly uninjured survivors, and one unfortunate victim, with tanned legs and a foot still attached to a white stiletto. The shoe was delicately fitted, though it missed its heel. A large, completely unblemished watermelon was also rescued. It all sadly felt like Cinderella without her pumpkin. Later, Allen retrieved Grace's heel from Yannis' pocket.

The official enquiry found no foul play or negligence despite Yannis and Christian's arguments. Yannis asserted that Christian had been smoking on board and that the hatch to the engine room had been opened but left unlocked, which it should not have been. He also stressed that despite the non-smoking policy on board, which was somewhat vague in the first place, he had witnessed Christian lighting a second cigar immediately after disposing of the first overboard. It was established that Grace had been seated near a open hatch and that the Meltemi wind had started to blow its breezy duty again when

Christian had hurled his first cigar stub overboard, still lit.

It was also established in the port marine engineer authorities report, who had witnessed the lengthy service and repairs done to the craft, that there had been a small fault on the main fuel line, which had been rectified prior to the boat's departure from the port. In accordance with Yannis's statement, the vessel had been determined sea worthy without a doubt. Christian countered, however, that both he and Grace had smelt fuel during the journey from the docking area in Itea and on the journey home. Socrates even confirmed the smell at Itea, and included that he had seen the engine room hatch open as his cousin had endeavoured to make adjustments whilst he, Grace, and Christian visited Delphi.

In attendance at the enquiry, joined by many of the locals eager to rubberneck, were a couple of magistrates from Athens, the British Embassy representative from Athens, and a senior British Police Officer, who had taken the opportunity to volunteer and take a holiday at the same time. In addition, the rescuers Finn and Alise Thompson, Her Majesty's Royal Diving Marines, fortunately not dressed in wetsuits for court, turned up to give evidence. A senior representative from Laskarina Holidays also came along with a grief counsellor called Daryl and a couple of court-approved translators for both Greek and English. Allen was there, of course, accompanied by the local priest, fortunately not Father Basil of Panagia Kastri Monastery. The local police officers Titus Spiros and Dikaios were present, but not required to provide testimony, only to control the crowd.

According to the Thompsons, the Boreas had approached Kea at considerable speed. They witnessed a huge explosion permeating from the craft's amidships and witnessed several large flying objects hurtling from the blast, one of which must have been Grace How-How-How-Unlucky-Houseman-Smith. Allen bet the Oracle didn't see that coming.

Proceeding with his account without a great deal of tact, Finn stated that the poor unfortunates had been on the last leg of their journey home. A few rather tasteless giggles where overheard in the assembly at the temporarily convened courthouse in the island's old Rex Cinema. Finn and Alise recalled they were about to take their second dive of the day from their inflatable with "Navy" stencilled on its side when they saw the explosion. They mentioned that the craft, the Boreas, sank within minutes, leaving burning matter on the water. They immediately fired up their boat, not in a Thompson machine-gun sort of way, but with a physical cranking of their RIB engine, to take them over to search the disaster area. They found Christian almost immediately, with a wet cigar still in his mouth and clutching a huge watermelon as a float. This was fortunate for him since he was not a good swimmer but also somewhat ironic as Grace had bought the thing.

Yannis was saved too, although his right arm had caught on fire and had to be extinguished. They searched desperately for Grace, using up the last of their oxygen supplies in a brave, but futile, attempt to find her. All that was discovered was one of her legs. The leg, which Finn had wrapped up in a black bin bag sealed with gaffer tape, was presented as evidence at the enquiry. Many onlookers vomited. Not a giggle, cough or suppressed laugh was to be heard again at the Rex Cinema during the proceedings. Grace's left leg and stiletto was transferred to a cold storage unit at the local mortuary, temporarily placed next to some frozen king prawns and a lobster, awaiting further instruction from the coroner.

The enquiry, after some deliberation, declared the unfortunate incident a tragedy and, in English law, death by misadventure. The manager of Laskarina and Christian exonerated Allen from all possible redress and responsibility for the tragic accident. Yannis's insurance company agreed to pay in full for the Boreas, and the manager of the holiday company promptly went home to the UK after the hearing. Finn and Alise were to be recognised for their bravery in the line of holiday duty.

36
A FUNERAL

Grace, of her maiden name Grace Sinitta Moor, was an only child. Sinitta is of Irish origin and means "Gift of God", who no doubt by now has the gift of Grace's pleasure, whether he wants it or not.

The coffin, slightly larger than an average shoe box and more like a boot box in appearance, was made of Greek olive wood and glazed with a white gloss finish, uncannily similar to Grace's stilettos. The undertakers had little to do in terms of make-over, just cleaning the leg, some leg wax and fake tan. They did, however, repair the shoe, refitting the heel Allen had given them. There was no question about the leg lying in state, so the coffin was sealed, decorated with white Athenian rose petals and finished with two brass handles that looked like they had come off a vintage chest of drawers. As the undertaker explained, it was all a question of scale. For a boxed leg, normal handles would have looked far too big, and as there was to be only one pallbearer required to solemnly carry the coffin, it simply wouldn't have looked right. Allen was surprised they hadn't fitted casters and a collapsible handle, suitcase style. He immediately felt stabbed as a heel. He felt guilty for imagining this.

Grace had by all accounts no other living family. Her mother, being the last survivor of the Moor linage, had passed away at the rather tactlessly named Peaceful Pasture Nursing Home in Basildon, Essex, five years before. Without any children or other living relative, Christian romantically decided to bury her leg on Kea, the rest of her body having been consumed by the Aegean Sea. It was agreed by all concerned that the funeral would be held at a beautiful old white chapel with a red dome near Loulida, the capital of the island. Grace's leg would be interred at the cemetery, very close to the Lion of Kea and just off the stone road from the Agios Spyridon Cathedral.

Father Thyme, literally named, and not for the herb or for his youthful appearance, was willing to perform the service in his trendy, modern, Greek Orthodox way. Christian chose the music, which

Allen agreed to play on his Yamaha DX7 keyboard. Allen was unsure whether the choice of "Amazing Grace" was sincere or an act of dark humour.

The church of Agia Marina stands next to the ruins of a Byzantine fort that towers above the seventeenth-century chapel. The window lintels to the church are painted blue and a single bell stands alone, suspended within an arched construction surmounted by a white crucifix. A natural spring of running fresh water flows nearby and nourishes the tall cypresses which, in the evening, throb to the cicadas' beat. The chapel is located about six kilometres from Loulida, going inland. Whilst "Agia" means "saint", which Grace certainly wasn't, Allen assumes "Marina" is related to water, which is appropriate here. It is, in fact, a female name taken from the Latin "Marinus", which coincidentally mean "of the sea". With the natural spring and Grace's unfortunate demise, no reference to water escaped Allen's attention.

It is surprising, at a funeral, how many friends a person has if, of course, they were still alive to enjoy their company. The poet Anthony turned up, wishing to read about death, but Allen tactfully declined his offer. The Crawfords came wearing their beanie hats. The Royal Marines, Finn and Alise, sporting pristine Green berets which Allen presumes they must take everywhere, march into the chapel. The goddess Saffy, with Kevin the Adonis, and Bret, all make an appearance, as did cigar-smoking Christian, with his newfound friend and business partner, the slightly scorched Yannis. In conversation, it was overheard that a new venture, about a water-borne cruising deal, was in the offing, using Christian's money, no doubt supplemented by Grace's life insurance policy. Mateo, who was organising the wake buffet, without forgetting the dolmades, at the Windy Bar, and Nikos, from pot removal and sewage systems, arrived together on an old moped, both wearing suits dusty from the road. Even Father Basil came from the monastery. Grace's hairdresser and Dikaios and Titus Spiros, in full police uniform, turned up too, along with many other Greek curious onlookers. The UK Police Chief was notable by his absence, choosing a day at the beach instead.

The inside of Agia Marina is beautiful and somewhat small, certainly too petite to accommodate all who have turned up to bear witness to Grace. It was built in a the shape of a cross. Its three main parts are the narthex, or vestibule, the nave, and the screened templon form the basic internal structure. The gilded quadriptych screen is older than the chapel and must have made its way to its present location from other sources. The religious iconography—not Sean Connery—is truly spectacular to behold—like Mr Connery himself. The velvet curtain, positioned centrally between the panels, is in dire need of a refurbishment, and the screen and curtain stand like a loyal guard over the simple stone altar behind. All the walls are painted white, with two giant frescoes adorning each side below the dome that suspends a huge, brass-cupped chandelier.

The chairs, all occupied, appear to be from olive wood or pitch pine, with padded red leather cushions. Father Thyme stands solemnly at the lectern, looking frequently at old Father Basil for reassurance. Allen leads Penne to her seat before taking a few short steps towards the amplifier. The keyboard sits on its stand, to the left of the screen by the altar. Allen realises this is his first gig in a church. He looks at Daryl, the grief counsellor standing next to him, dreadlocks and all, holding a pink twelve-string guitar. Allen hopes he doesn't play "Oh Happy Day", it simply wouldn't be appropriate with all its invitation to wash away one's sins.

The service began with young Father Thyme giving Allen the nod. In response, the crowd, both indoors and outdoors, fell silent. Allen, supported by Daryl on the guitar, started to play "Amazing Grace" as Christian entered in a short-sleeved Hawaiian shirt covered in printed yellow hibiscus flowers. He walked up the nave with Grace, her boxed leg placed rather clumsily on the bier which was far too big for such a small coffin. A simple wreath of white roses and laurel slid from the top of her coffin and landed on the flag-stoned floor in a disarranged mess. Christian replaced them the best he could for someone who had no skills in flower arrangements.

At the lectern, Father Thyme gestured Christian to the last remaining seat. He promptly tripped over Alise's feet and fell onto the old ones of the Crawfords. Regrettably, one of the eulogy candles fell over, dripping hot wax on Denholm. Father Thyme cleared his throat, looking for reassurance from Father Basil, who nodded his head in assent. The accident was briefly cleaned and then the service resumed.

'Death is an inevitable part of being human, but we're never really prepared when it happens to someone we…loved.' Someone was heard coughing.

37
The cemetery and committal

The service took longer than usual due to the need for translation and the echoes from the external speakers erected for those outside. Back to the Lion of Kea and the adjacent cemetery just off the stone road to Loulida, it was decided a hearse would be too much for one leg, so Christian placed Grace's remains in the boot of the Marines' blacked-out, air-conditioned Range Rover. The military, back home, had loaned the car for the twins to use on Kea.

A small yet properly dug hole in the dry ground has been marked as Grace's final residence on earth. The spot has been chosen beneath the shade of an ancient olive tree which prospered well with ripe fruit. The coffin was lowered gently into the ground until one of the white ribbons slipped its lowering bow, flooring the coffin with a dull thud. Father Thyme uttered a timeless prayer and Christian chucked in some soil and, accidentally, the ash of his cigar's end.

'She wouldn't have minded,' he coughed. 'One thing she always had was a weird sense of humour.'

Christian had ordered a modest stone, which was to be set when the ground beneath had hardened. Unlike many of the large and strangely beautiful monuments in the cemetery, Grace's stone was a modest affair. It had been purchased in Athens, using Christian's gold American Express card via the local undertaker. Made from white marble with two cherubs, it remains interesting nonetheless with its simple inscription: her name, birth date, death date, and a three-word epitaph cut deep into the stone: "Child of God". A CD by some Welsh male choir plays a harmonious rendition of "For Those in Peril on the Sea", whilst the mourners depart, wondering what sandwiches will be at the wake and if souvlaki will be on the menu.

A strange convoy of mopeds, vans, Mercedes, and two mini tractors, led by the Marines' Range Rover, make their way to the Windy Bar. Allen takes Penne, Anthony, Bret, Saffron, and Kevin in the company bus. The Crawfords, Denholm still complaining about his scorched pink cotton jacket, rather inappropriate for a funeral, drive themselves in their Fantasy Car. There is little traffic on Kea. In fact, the present stone road constitutes more of a rally akin to one at a local election on the island.

With the Windy Bar in view, the convoy parks up. Mateo is first up the low stairs, at some pace to the bar by the pool. The tables still look neatly set, but the cats, led by an orange-eared specimen, have helped themselves to the dolmades which have been neglectfully left on top of the unlit, brick barbecue. Fortunately, the kitchen door has remained closed, and the beasts have not gained access to the fridges where the sandwiches, vol-au-vents and souvlaki where temporarily stored.

Mateo ignites the barbecue, which singes his bushy eyebrows slightly as he attempts to grab the old, orange-eared cat with the intent to chuck the sod on the smoking wood and coals. He fails, so no cat on the menu.

'May I indulge you all with my own very personal eulogy to Grace, now?' Anthony announces. He has, as usual, already consumed a skin full.

'Is it clean?' Allen asks him. 'And will it translate well for all our dear Greek friends here?'

'Totally, old boy!'

The crowd, still munching, and conversations, still flowing, stop when Mateo announces that Anthony is about to perform a reading.

'It's called "Death".'

Allen whispers to Anthony, 'Respect please.'

'It's called "Respect Death".' Slurs Anthony between hiccups.

Death

I twist my body so,
to be your strength and cradle.
To place a healing hand,
to stroke away the grief.
To chase out this darkest night and day,
to dry these burning salty tears.
But I am no God,

nor a healer for a resurrection.
I cannot ease such infinite pain,
or stop the perpetual clock,
to turn back its shadow hands.
I cannot blow a cold wind warm,
or make a desert bloom,
with primula and daffodils.
But what I do hold firm
is a soft and tender kiss.
A simple easy touch,
given with all my heart and hope within.
In certain blessed truth with all I am,
and all that I may be.
With all I have to share,
in life and in death.
and in all that simply is.
This memory of you,
cherished of you,
For us,
You.

'I wrote that for my dear wife Annita. She died of bowel cancer four years ago,' croaks the poet. 'The name Annita means "grace unguided", how ironic is that?'

The Meltemi blows again, shaking the awning and lifting a plastic cup from the bar, interrupting the silence. Seconds pass in complete quiet that even the orange-eared cat sits in silence on the stone wall until a rapturous applause breaks out. The poet sobs a dry old tear and requests another Ouzo.

'Fucking deep, that!' Allen whispers to Penne, whose mascara has smudged her face.

'Fucking deep, indeed.' Both overwhelmed by the situation, they forget the drowning implications within the misplaced comment.

'Want to hear my tribute, now?' Denholm Crawford pipes up, also legless, but in an alcohol-induced way. 'It's in the form of a song. I'm afraid my vocal tone may be a tad flat…'

Margaritte looks at him with deep suspicion and a little dread.

Denholm's karaoke skills are not the best. He promptly bursts into the classic Welsh country, Western style, song by Andy Fairweather Low. The song is inappropriately named "Wide Eyed and Legless". Margaritte Crawford knows the song and punches him firmly in the gut, which regrettably causes the copious amounts of black olives he has consumed to be returned on the paper tablecloth. One of the home-grown olives catches in his throat and causes him a severe chocking fit.

First aider extraordinaire Bret is straight in, biceps flexed. He hurls the Crawford's table out of the way, sending it to land with a splash into the swimming pool, exuding olive residue into the crystal water. He grabs Denholm from behind and starts lifting and shaking him. The stuck olive frees itself and Denholm collapses on the floor.

Summoning up what is left of his previous composure, he stands somewhat unsteadily, and adds through the gasps, 'Sorry, I've gone and done it again,' which is coincidentally one of the lines from the song.

Penne looks at Allen. 'Fancy some sex? We seriously run the risk of being injured if we stay here too long.'

'Too right, hon,' he agrees. 'We're out of here, just don't wear the PVC boots today.'

38
A Strange Occurrence

Mateo assures Allen that he will get Anthony home to his villa next door and kindly gives the loved-up couple a superb takeaway consisting of a varied selection of leftovers, including a couple of complimentary bottles of red and white wines.

Allen realises he has forgotten to take his medication for the past two days. He considers taking them or not, both fearing the complications if he doesn't take them and the possibilities if he does, or the possibilities if he doesn't and the complications if he does. He certainly needs to take those for the blood pressure. Everything is an overly complex dilemma when he has just buried a leg, has mental health issues and is craving sex.

In a lover's post-coital embrace, he raises himself on one arm from the unfashionably untidy but dangerously comfortable sheets, to pass Penne her French cigarettes. Smoking in bed is a dangerous habit, almost suicidal, but then this is Grace ... Greece. He sips his chilled white Gonidakis, a local wine from the nearby island of Kythnos.

'What a day, and that was top.'

'Which part?' Penne replies dreamily.

'Well, all of it really, apart from the funeral and the wake. Did I break that bedside lamp, in one of our more adventurous moments of bliss?'

'Allen...' Penne raises a manicured eyebrow. 'You really are the only person I know who could combine sex with funerals and light fittings and still make it sound like a compliment.'

'Thanks Penn. It's my fault if it's fucked, but my mother gave it to me years ago back in the UK before she died. It's not real Art Nouveau but the thing is kind of sentimental.'

Penne kisses him then reaches over to the collapsed bedside table beside him. His phone and the lamp have both fallen on the floor. Allen admires her beautiful naked butt as she inspects the damage.

'No, all okay. Nothing broken that I can see, so it can't have been made in China. Your phone looks sick though.'

'Fuck the phone, all it does is bring me grief. You sure the lamp is okay?'

'One hundred percent fine. Even the shade isn't chipped.'

'I'll unplug it just in case.'

After unplugging the lamp, he goes to open the shutters. The sky is pristine, clear through the dark, and the moon is bright and full. The smell of bread and wine lingers as the stars weave and shimmy like a million fireflies. The gentle breeze drifts in to clear the heady scent of sex and waves the white voile drapes.

It is three am, the death hour, when the grim reaper stalks his prey with gardening tools. All is quiet and only the insomniacs and the young teens are awake. Penne is roused from sleep, feeling slightly alarmed and very cold. One of the bedroom shutters creaks and moves with the wind, exploring the open window. It knocks its casing with a regular rhythm causing a gently snoring Allen to turn, gasp, and turn again in the bed. The temperature drops further and Penne, still naked, her beautiful body silhouetted by the moon, closes the shutters and locks them with the old wrought iron handles. She closes the windows for good measure, locking them too even though the time of year dictates otherwise. She creeps back into bed with care not to wake Allen. She feels irrational, and slightly uneasy. She adjusts the summer duvet to cover her breasts, realising how scared she is. Gently, she prods Allen's back but only to obtain a vague response and more snoring. His arm falls loosely from the bed but he remains fast asleep. Until, of course, his phone rings.

'What the fuck?' He shouts, waking up as if from a car crash.

'It's your phone, hon.'

'What bloody time is it?'

'Oh, about three thirty in the morning.'

'Who the fuck rings at three thirty in the morning?'

Allen knows even before the question is raised that it can only be unwelcome news at this hour. He reaches across her, promptly falling off of the bed. The phone continues its irritating jingle until he finds it, face down, underneath the collapsed bedside table drawer. It should have gone into voice mail by now. He flips it over where he notices the green display is fractured. The caller ID still remains persistent and legible. It reads, in capital letters "THE DEVIL".

Allen immediately drops the phone like it is a hot potato, confused, shocked, and in a state of disbelief. Despite the obvious damage, it continues to ring. He picks it up, slides back the chrome housing, and holds it with a shaking hand to his ear.

A vague hint of wind drifts through the static fizz of the air waves and the sound of some far away house party permeates through the white noise. A giggle, an infant's gurgle, breaks through and then far, far away, way back, almost indiscernible, he hears what sounds like that unmistakable squeal. "Alleeeen!" What worries Allen the most is the broken and unclear words that come next. "See you later. It's all okay here."

'Who was it?' Penne asks, now sitting upright in bed, discerningly worried.

'I, I, simply don't know…' Allen stutters, looking at the phone now dead in his hand. 'I just don't understand but it sounded very much like Grace. I need a drink, Pen'

'Its four forty in the morning, darling!'

'I don't care, it's either a drink or a tranquillizer.'

'Alright, I'll get the brandy.'

39
The Crawfords

'We were big in biscuits once, don't you know? Although my ambition would love to have included the invention of the Hobnob. Bloody McVitie's! Our crackers are still on top with a bit of Double Gloucester or Stilton.' Denholm tells Dikaios at the police station.

It should be noted that Crawford's Biscuits originally opened as a small shop owned by William Crawford near Leith, Edinburgh, in 1813. The company expanded, and opened its Fairfield Biscuit works in Old Swan, Liverpool, in 1897, and became one of Liverpool's main employers. The company stayed in the family until Denholm sold out to United Biscuits in the sixties, who took with them Mcvitie's to complete UB's global cookie domination and urban nutritional munching portfolio. Crawford's early advertising straplines, "Great Value Everyday Biscuits", and "Crawford's Biscuits are the Best", remained for many years, as did their products, Custard Creams, Jam Rings and the mighty Digestive. Denholm and Margaritte Crawford, currently in their own sort of custard at Loulida Police Station, are testament to this sweet and crunchy biscuit legacy.

Allen has been summoned on the semi-busted phone. 'What! Did I hear that correctly? You're both in the slammer?' He is in disbelief, his blood pressure in free fall.

'Well, no it's not me, Denholm's the one in trouble.'

'What in God's name for?'

'Watercolour painting, unfortunately…' She replies sheepishly.

'You've been arrested for painting? Bloody painting!'

'Yes, Allen, we're sorry. We artists have always suffered for our art.'

'I'll be right over. Just don't panic.'

It is two in the afternoon. They must have consumed all that brandy last night. 'Bloody hell!'

Watercolour painting is a delicate art medium. Many purists and art snobs think it remains the pastime of the amateur pensioner, although this is completely inaccurate. See J.M.W. Turner. Watercolour, or "aquarelle" in French, is derived from the Latin "aqua", again inappropriate considering Grace's watery tomb. It requires a dexterity of touch that is both soft, yet direct, positive, but contradictorily vague, and difficult to remove if a mistake from a misplaced brush stroke is left. A bit like drumming. If the drummer cocks up, everyone in the audience will hear it. The art of watercolour relies immensely on the application of tinted washes using sable hair, brushes of varied size, and complex stroke techniques. Unlike oil or acrylic when one can just paint over the damage, unless of course it has been applied with a builder's trowel. One uncertain move with a watercolour and the whole thing is basically ruined.

Which is exactly what Denholm and Margaritte have done with sun cream. Whether due to the application of the lotion by Margaritte or the blazing sun on Denholm's naked body, the cause for Denholm's aged erection is up for debate. The timing was unfortunate as it happened to occur following Dikaios' patrol in the police car.

'Gross indecency is a major public offence, Allen,' Titus states in a pompous, official way whilst nodding his head at Dikaios's report. 'In fact, a total disgrace.'

'They were only attempting to paint. Actually, their work is rather good.'

'There is painting and there is painting. If you do some DIY, Allen, it's normally with overalls, and without a naked erection.'

'Look, buddy,' Allen is at the very edge of patience, 'this is Greece. Just walk down the street to your local tobacco and newspaper stand, ouzo-filled glass statuettes of various erected male appendages are on sale. I rather doubt poor Mr Crawford's is that big, and I don't suppose he, or his manhood, was engaged in any position that the local tobacco vendor sells in his books depicting the images of sex in Ancient Greece. For God's sake, man, he must be in his late seventies! He deserves a medal rather than penalization!' Allen clears his throat. 'Forgive the pun. I strongly recommend you release my client immediately. Read the book I mentioned or, if you can't read, at least look at the pictures. Sun cream or not, the guy is hardly the great John Curtis Holmes!'

Allen shrugs in despair. 'What exactly happened, Mrs Crawford?'

'Well, we were attempting to do some life drawing and I needed the figure in the frame so I could complete the image later whilst capturing the background. I needed a model and dear Denholm agreed. Possibly due to your nude cruising trip to the beach, Allen.' Titus raises an eyebrow. 'And with the heat, I think he may have become a little excited. You know, the breeze, the lotion to stop him burning and all. Frankly, I haven't seen him like that since the mid-seventies.'

'Do you have the picture Mrs Crawford?'

'What, of Denholm's penis?'

Allen clarifies. 'No, the background.'

'Yes, dear, it's here.' She searches in an old leather satchel full of original pictures. 'Found it!' She hands the picture over, which is beautifully constructed.

It features the unpainted Denholm sitting astride a large rock. Allen notes the background, it is superb. He knows the place where the image has been crafted. He also observes the outline of Mr Crawford, with what looks like a good size, unpainted object, jutting out from his lower regions.

'That really is very, very, good, Mrs Crawford. Would you consider putting on an exhibition here on the island? That may get us out of here, but no nudes, okay?'

'Absolutely, dear! Truly, I would be delighted and more than a little honoured.'

A deal is brokered with the police and Denholm, still naked but covered in a sheet, is released. Thankfully the sun cream has been absorbed and the erection is no more.

40
Fool's gold

A man and his wealth are easily separated, but a man with his dreams of wealth are also easily disappointed. As Macbeth says, "Here's a farmer that hang'd himself on the expectation of plenty," presumably after an unpredicted drought, followed by perpetual rain. In reality, then, a normal British summer. Fortunately for Finn and Alise, both on healthy expense accounts, their expectations are comfortably reassured. Their sponsors, in a semi unofficial and very clandestine capacity, are both the Greek and British governments, working together in agreement, for once, and without a mention of the disputed Parthenon Marbles.

Allen returns to his apartment to find Penne reading *Far from the Madding Crowd* printed in Greek. She is sitting on the balcony next to Russell the lemon tree. 'Good day at the office, dear?'

'That novel should be called "Far from the Maddening Tourists".'

Allen leans over and kisses her, then proceeds to inform her on the crazy Crawfords and the forthcoming watercolour exhibition.

'Good news is, my phone still works. Although after last night's call, I'm unsure whether I shouldn't take the wretched SIM card out.'

'That was all so screwed up and weird,' she confirms, taking a large gulp of cranberry juice.

'Is there vodka in that?' He asks, pointing to her glass.

'What? After all that brandy?'

'The naked painting adventures today really call for a Sea Breeze, and I am definitely not talking about the Meltemi here. Do we have any grapefruit juice in the fridge? Do you want one?'

'Go on then, sex doll, I'm in. But we don't have grapefruit.'

'No matter, just throw me one of Russell's lemons and say sorry to him.'

He concocts the drinks and brings them out onto the balcony.

'Bliss, heavenly bliss!'

He twirls the ice in his highball glass and looks at Penne in her black bikini. 'You are one hot girlfriend.'

'*Fiancée*, boy!' She laughs, holding out her ringed finger in a sort of black power salute.

But Allen's phone rings again with its usual optimal timing. No contact details are visible on the cracked display, so he lets it ring. He looks at Penne, who motions her hand to a sign of compliant acceptance.

Allen answers, expecting the worst, but is pleasantly surprised by the voice on the end of the line.

'It's the marines.' He mouths.

'How are you man?' Finn barks with his usual gruff tone. 'We need some more O2. We used all of our supply trying to salvage that Grace woman.'

'Have you tried the sky?'

'Don't be a clever sod, Allen, we like you, but we don't tolerate smart arses.'

'I kind of figured that out already. Try Kea Divers, Koundouraki Beach. You need to talk to Moses Jones. Oh and he's not the same guy who parted the Red Sea, before you ask." He searches through all the paperwork and fliers wedged in a kitchen drawer for MJ's number at the Scuba Diving School. 'How is the diving going by the way? Found anything of interest yet?'

'Allen, we are not at liberty to discuss this and it's really none of your bloody business.'

'Just curious that's all, it's called conversation,' he replies cockily.

'You know what they say about curious people?' He adds in a commando way.

'Yep,' replies Allen, 'consider my intervention closed,' he confirms a tad pompously, after relaying MJ's contact details to Finn. The Marine promptly terminates the call.

Some of the history of the ill-fated HMHS Britannic, His Majesty's hospital ship, has already been told, but without too much elaboration on Finn and Alise's request. The vessel had been requisitioned for the Royal Navy. It had been repainted white with large red crosses and a horizontal green stripe from bow to stern and had set sail from Southampton in November 1916 amidst the death and turmoil of the First World War. It had been designed, like the Titanic, to be unsinkable. That was until it had struck a floating mine from the Imperial German Navy. It sank within fifty-five minutes, helped by the fact that all the portholes had been opened to assist the sick Australian and New Zealand soldiers on board. Fresh air being good for the health, the same as bullets and bombs. It was eight in the morning, breakfast time, bon-bombs, Scott's Porage Oats, and of course Indian tea. This was on the morning of the sixteenth, and many seriously-injured men and women were saved. That is after having incurred further injury from the explosion and the shrapnel from the blast. All before breakfast.

They were transported to Piraeus, whilst the victims who could walk remained on Kea, entertained at the hospitality of the brave and kind locals who rescued all they could. Thirty poor souls died and sank along with an unconfirmed secret cargo of gold. The mighty ship sank some four miles off the coastline of Kea with a hole in its side some twenty to thirty feet wide, and ten feet below the waterline, letting in the glorious Aegean Sea. The gold had travelled under the cover of the Red Cross and the poor injured Australian and New Zealander troops. The ANZAC, who had practised their landings for Gallipoli on Lemnos Island, and after the carnage of the battle at Gallipoli, were sent back to Lemnos to recover and heal their injuries before returning to the UK to ultimately continue with the further slaughter in the trenches of Northern France once healed.

The location of the gold remains a mystery. But should it be there and is willing to be found around one hundred and nine meters down, unlikely to be near the wreck at all, Finn and Alise will find it. According to the ship's faded inventory at the UK Ministry of Defence, the gold had been safeguarded in a wooden container, stencilled in black letters reading "Medical Supplies" and, ironically, "Handle with care".

41
Wednesday

More tourists on and more tourists off, back to Piraeus and the Ellinikon International Airport. Two departures from the hotel. Two new sets of arrivals, one of them being a family of three staying at the Villa Arum, which has been unoccupied for most of the season due to faulty plumbing and electrics that have now been fixed. The villa remains close to Mateo's Windy Bar, but stands above it on a rocky outcrop, with the wretched goats and the bar nestling scenically below. Its present occupiers include Ferdinand North, his wife Isabella, and their son Montgomery, plus a couple of chickens that come with the property and do not mind faulty plumbing. A small winding path leads down from the villa, through Mateo's knackered gate, and on to the bar's terrace and pool. Ferdinand is an antique dealer and B list media celebrity with his considerable skills offered to various media antique shows.

All the other current holiday-makers are accounted for, with the exception of Grace Houseman-Smith. Christian, however, has decided to stay, and is now renting a villa owned by his newfound friend Yannis up high in the hills. He should have been on the day's journey home with Grace, but it seems he has found in Yannis a soul and business friend. So he stays on the island, awaiting personal financial news from Athens and a newly-ordered quad bike. Thankfully he is no longer Allen's responsibility.

Young Monty seems to fulfil the nursery rhyme that Wednesday's child is "full of woe" with maximum potential. He is twelve, but brimming with teenage angst of someone much older. He is slightly overweight and, sadly, quite obnoxious as Allen discovers when he throws a wobbly after Allen refuses to stop the van at the local tobacco store. Presumably, Monty's requirements, at twelve, were not tobacco, but more high-calorie substances that his mother flatly refuses to allow him. By consequence, he sulks all the way to the Villa Arum and, upon arrival, jumps out of the van and slams the door. He then proceeds to kick an old chicken. Fortunately, he misses, concluding that he is no athletic sports man, if in fact chicken kicking was a registered sport, unlike curling on ice, for instance. But Allen certainly knows chicken flicking is not. Ask Colonel Sanders. Monty is a nasty little sod and probably a potential serial killer, or a potential serial chicken killer. His private education at Wardskip College, a hideous, huge, cold, Gothic Victorian monstrosity, or fee paying "remand home" is surrounded by Lumber Park. The institution is probably not helping the poor lad's physiological needs. On the upside, it does possess a truly beautiful and long drive planted on either side with old chestnut trees that are sadly wasted on their ultimate destination; namely the draconian school.

His dad, Ferdinand North, by contrast to his son, is a tall, educated, and lean man with slick black hair and modestly proportional diamond earring studs, somewhat resembling Al Pacino without the scarred face. He is dressed in a slightly flamboyant way with loose-fitting cream suits on brown leather espadrilles. His wife Isabella is petite, attractive, and powerful. She is wearing heavy ethnic silver jewellery that must have caused security a nightmare at the airport and, like her husband, she wears espadrilles, but in red, to match her summer flower dress covered in printed red roses. Allen really hopes there will be no more problems. This family seems possibly okay, with perhaps the exception of Montgomery North.

42
Oxygen and ice cream

Following another exhausting introductory tour, this time at the Hotel Hydra, Allen returns to the comparative tranquillity of Mateo's bar. It is lunchtime, and he and Penne share a bowl of fresh deep-fried calamari with tzatziki. Moses Jones, from the Scuba Diving School, arrives just after two in the afternoon with the oxygen supplies for the marines, twelve tanks of the stuff. He orders a beer and joins Allen and Penne who have just finished their lunch. No one quite knows where MJ comes from and no one dares asking, but he looks the part. Tall, muscular, with eyes almost black that show little emotion except perhaps kindness. He has shoulder-length dreadlocks tied back and wears sunglasses that look Italian by design. He high-fives Allen as he sits down.

'Respect. So what's happening, bro, this is a shit load of O2! And who's the babe? She's hot.'

'My fiancée. Oops sorry, man. *Ma'am.*' He holds out a huge hand to Penne, which swallows her small yet firm grip. 'Have they found anything yet? I tell you, the gold's a myth, man, I've hunted for years for it. All I came up with was an empty Greek amphora and a case of aged Glenfiddich. Well, I think it was Glenfiddich… I drank all the stuff.'

Montgomery appears through Mateo's gate. He looks dehydrated and slightly burnt. 'You ok, son?' Allen shouts.

'Fuck off, a sodding goat tried to head butt me.'

Undeterred, Allen yells. 'Call Mateo. He's out the back trying to repair the goat you kicked.' Allen's unsure how someone can "repair" a goat but concludes that some veterinary skills are required. 'He'll fix you up an ice cream or something.'

'It's not the something I want,' mouths Monty. 'Maybe a tequila sunrise or at least three fingers of vodka on ice.' Allen notes another benefit of a probable private education. Montgomery's sweaty fist is clutched tightly around a large wad of money. It is only three in the afternoon.

The poet Anthony remains fast asleep in his chair. His book and pack of black pens have fallen on the ground. He frankly looks very comfortable in his present position, back turned on the sea view but facing the far end of the pool, with a parasol rigged up to his chair that Mateo has made him. The gate appears closed. It is the same gate Monty will take on the path home to his parent's villa above.

Finn and Alise arrive in their large black and somewhat sinister vehicle to collect the oxygen. Allen has previously called them just after Moses arrived. The latter confirmed he wasn't taking his vehicle, "up that fucking dangerous dirt track to their villa". But he did say that he would help load the bottles off the van at the Windy Bar, which was sort of halfway.

'Pay me cash though, okay? US dollars preferably, if you have any, or pounds, no drachma.' He specifies. 'The school is now out of O2 and I've had to bust my ass to get a shit load delivered from Athens.'

Whilst he sorts the business between MJ and the marines, Anthony is still snoring and Penne reclines on a sun lounger. Monty is chatting with Mateo at the bar under the awning, having secured himself a bar stool. He's drinking, more than eating, vanilla ice cream mixed with vodka, a single shot, topped with a maraschino cherry, although Mateo's shots do not conform to British licensing standards. He is a generous man. A distant exhaust can be overheard teasing the tranquillity of a glorious afternoon. The wind blows and the sea is so very calm, so very blue. A small gecko basks in the sun on the old stone wall that surrounds the bar below the white canvas sail. Monty laughs at something Mateo has said, the comment probably being X-rated. The poet's straw hat is blown from his head, which Penne retrieves before it falls into the pool. She re-adjusts it on Anthony's aged temple, rousing him slightly, before quickly drifting back to a deep slumber.

The sound of what could be a Honda NX650 Dominator comes into view surrounded by dust from the stone road. An old blue moped follows it at some distance, desperately trying to keep up with the Honda. The vehicles make their way noisily towards the bar, none of the riders wearing a helmet. Saffron's hair billows behind her and Kevin, whose tan has become about three shades darker since Allen saw him last, dismounts politely after her. She is wearing micro shorts and a tight white tee-shirt with "I am Spartacus" printed in black. The statement is slightly distorted by her nipples. Kevin's dress style is slightly strange. He is wearing Harley Davidson ankle boots with short, black Bermuda shorts and a white vest top. They seem to wait for the other rider before entering the bar. Bret arrives on his bike, blowing heavy, dark exhaust fumes. He appears to have more scars on his face and a relatively new, fresh-looking graze to his knee. He swears at the moped before chucking it across Mateo's parking area. He is also wearing black with a shirt that reads "Five Degrees West" in white and a matching bandana complemented by a pair of traditional Greek sandals.

'Fantastic safety wear for bikes on these roads!' Allen shouts.

Bret picks up his moped, nods at Allen and parks it upright next to the Dominator.

'Fell off the bastard two days ago getting groceries. Bust the eggs and my face. Fantasy Cars my ass. I thought we should visit for some late lunch. Nothing with eggs in, though, or carbon monoxide.' He adds dryly, looking at the smoking moped with hatred.

Monty pays his bill, tips Mateo handsomely, then slips from his bar stool, straining his ankle.

'The vodka,' he states somewhat sheepishly, or more aptly, goatishly. Allen is slightly worried about his vodka-ice cream consumption at twelve years old. He salutes the marines, both of whom admirably return the compliment, then makes his rather unsteady exit to the gate at the rear of the terrace that leads back up the hill to his villa above.

The marines pull across another table and mismatched chairs. Saffy sits next to Allen facing the pool while Penne sits to his left.

'A rose between two thorns,' Finn jokes as he takes a seat opposite him with Bret and Kevin. Alise takes the end seat and Mateo brings more tablecloths. Somewhat forgotten about, Anthony remains asleep by the pool, shaded by the parasol and the mighty Moses takes the last remaining seat at the other end of the table. Mateo brings out the bread, two big jugs of white wine, olives, and a paper pad to take the order. Calamari is the big seller, as is the local goat burger with cheese, ham, and pickled gherkins. Penne also orders red apples cut into quarters with a glass of Calvados. The Meltemi is still blowing as the gate gently eases open after Monty's departure, unnoticed.

'To Grace.' Alise announces unexpectedly. They all assemble and raise their drinks. 'Yamas! I do not know this to be true but, in Greece, I believe if you clink the top of a glass it means there will either be a fight, or something predestined will go wrong so always clink at the bottom.' He winks at Kevin.

'I think I've heard that before!' Interjects Saffy as the gate opens wider. 'I've certainly clinked Kevin's bottom!'

'Too much information.' Bret interrupts.

The sun remains glorious and present all over. Allen and Penne are listening to the tune of distant goat bells heard quite clearly above Mateo's sound system that plays the Cures' "Caterpillar". Allen remembers the forgotten blood pressure pills and all the other crap medication he apparently needs to calm his brain box, none of which seems to work anyway.

A sudden gust of marine air sets the gate free, swinging gently like a magician's hand before the finale at the end of a trick. "Now you see it, now you do not." The sleight of a hand, maybe Monty's, remains unnoticed. The first goat to go through is a big, angry-looking white buck with twisted horns. It breaks free from the scrub land and gains instant access to the terrace. The sod, clearly the leader of the pack, is followed by a couple of shaggy brown accomplices through the swinging gate. It jams wide open just as food is being served. The rest of the herd, some thirty beasts or so, play follow the leader and all hell breaks out. It is a campanologist's nightmare, bells ringing everywhere to no tune or key. The white sod charges through, clearly undaunted by Mateo's dining guests, followed closely by Bonnie and Clyde the shaggy twins. Despite the bells and the sound of stampeding hooves, Anthony does not wake up, having consumed a light breakfast and lunch, and half a bottle of ouzo, a truly marvellous remedy for insomnia. The situation is turning into a sort of classic western, except with goats as the cattle and no lasso.

The white buck initiates a full-frontal assault on the poor poet in his chair, which the strange beast regards as some territorial threat. He gets one spiralled horn stuck in the mechanisms of the wheeled apparatus, whilst his two aides push on. The rest of the tribe invades the bar, hunting for the fresh Calamari, some of the goat burgers, ironically, and the paper tablecloths. They wash it all down with copious amount of spilt wine. A black and white beast, coincidentally called Lassie, and looks like a mini Friesian but with tactile horns, even manages to get its head stuck through the handle of a jug. "Jughead", "Judge Dredd", "Jarhead" are all phrases that enter Allen's tired mind as he observes the white buck, aka the Lone Ranger, pull Anthony, the parasol, and his chair, into the deep end of the pool.

'There's a goat in my pool! What am I gonna do?' Mateo yells.

'And a fucking poet!' Penne adds.

Allen is the first to react. He barges two goats and a table out of the way with his shoulder, like an American footballer but without the layered padding and helmet. Rugby Union is the only football game Allen likes, a bit of insulation tape round the forehead and the game is on. Certainly not the suit of armour that disappeared in the middle ages in jousting. He and Alise, without taped heads but fully clothed, jump in the pool, ignoring the "No diving allowed" sign. The buck is attempting to find the shallow end but Anthony is sinking straight to the bottom. The men get hold of him and bring him back to the surface, hatless and without the wheelchair. Kevin jumps in to retrieve the rest: the chair, the hat, and the parasol.

Penne has picked up Anthony's goat-trampled book when Mateo and Saffron were herding the goats back into the scrub land behind the Windy Bar, fixing the gate behind them. She looks at the manuscript that the poet had obviously been writing. Its title reads *Colourfield*. On first impression, it appears to be a children's story, which intrigues Penne, and she starts to read.

Colourfield

Daddy Black was the first colour in the world, and probably in the great scheme of things will be the last as well. To be perfectly accurate, he was not really a colour at all, as there was nothing else out there to compare him to. So he remained in the great scheme of things a colour, the only colour.

One day after millions and millions of years in endless darkness,

Daddy Black realised he was, in truth, very, very, lonely.

'I need family, friends, a companion, someone to share a life with.' He announced to the big black empty spinning vortex around him. 'Someone to care for, and someone to care for me.'

By a wondrous divine achievement and certainly after much considered thought—and a miracle—, he created a child. A son. Someone not too far removed from the colour black. The Boy Blue.

Daddy Black and Boy Blue played long and fine for many happy years until, ultimately, on yet another blackish, blueish drab day, the Boy Blue announced:

'We need more friends, Dad. I need a friend of my own, a friend as good as you but a friend who is, how do I say this… a little younger perhaps.'

As if by magic, the vortex erupted. The blue-black sky folded in on itself and a big, glowing ball of fire appeared. A perfect Pearl, too dazzling even to look at, appeared. A Pearl so bright, so powerful, so warm, that it caused Blue to step back in awe. He rubbed his eyes and shaded them with his hands, watching the light spill through his fingers to caress his face. The glorious light bobbed and spun in front of him, radiating wellness, so bright, so new.

'Hello,' said Blue, nervous but excited at the same time. 'Will you be my friend? May I name you something? May I call you Sun, after me? I do hope we can be friends?'

The big yellow Pearl paused her dance in the vortex and hovered close to Boy Blue. 'I will call you Yellow is that ok?'

'De…Lighted,' said Yellow Sun. 'But I will have to ask my mum, Mummy White, first.

Daddy Black and Mummy White discussed long and hard the prospects for Yellow Sun and Boy Blue becoming friends, and whilst the parents immediately liked each other, they made reasons for, and excuses against, why the two should not be together. The conversation included many fine words like "love", "probably", "possibly", even "maybe", followed by the final word, "perhaps". At which point Grey appeared.

Grey pointed his small, wrinkled hand and said, 'Let them be! See how well they play together. Look now, Daddy Black and Mummy White, look to the ground!'

Mummy White and Daddy Black looked to the ground below as Yellow Sun and Boy Blue played and ever-so-slowly a new colour began to form. It filled the field growing beneath them.

'Oh my!' What is all this?' Whispered Mummy White, scared but excited too.

'We call this Green,' replied Yellow Sun and Boy Blue as one.

'Green will be the colour of our home!' Blue continued. 'See how at peace and good it all is now and look, look now to these mighty growing things, Daddy!'

Daddy Black looked at the growing things.

'They are trees.' Said Yellow Sun. And sure enough, blossoms seemed to appear on the newborn boughs and then were gone.

'What now?' He asked, clearly impressed.

'Look!' Boy Blue shouted. 'Look at Green!' The first of many ripe apples started to form on the branches atop the leaves. 'We will call them Red.'

'Red. Red Apples,' Yellow Sun adds.

Anthony splutters on chlorinated water as Bret massaged and pumped his chest.

'Look red, red, apples!' Anthony shouts pointing at Penne's uneaten bowl of fruit. 'Red pissing apples. Read the words, read the God damn words!' He coughs, vomiting up pool water. 'Red fucking, bastard apples. I haven't had one of them since the late seventies, or a swim for that matter.' 'Everyone okay?' Asks a soaked Anthony. 'Did the water get that bastard goat?'

'Regrettably, no.' Allen answers, also soaked and not quite feeling fine. A pain grips his chest, distracting him from the present.

'Shame. That goat is a bloody killer! The sooner Mateo gets him on a burger with some cheese and onion, the better.'

Penne hands him the wet, hoof-marked sheets. 'Your manuscript.'

'You read it, you actually read it?' Anthony asks.

'Yes,' replies Penne. 'And furthermore, it's hauntingly good.'

'"Hauntingly good". I like that!' He considers, trying to write down the prose but finding the paper too soaked. 'I wish I could find an agent or publisher to say the same. They're all mainly scared prats, you know, until one fucker hits on you and then of course it's

Groundhog Day but in reverse.'

'What is "ground dog"? Mateo asks politely. 'Is it like a goat? Maybe oriental even?'

Penne looks at Allen holding his chest. He looks back at her, but she is now looking at Finn, who is looking at Bret, who appears somewhat exhausted. Bret looks at his drenched friend Kevin, and Kevin looks back at him and then at Saffy, who in turn, looks at her bosom and then at Alise, who looks at Kevin's wet tee-shirt with interest. They all look almost at once at the sodden poet.

'No, no, no, Mateo!' Allen says. 'It's too complex to explain... It's an American thing.'

'Ah,' responds Mateo. 'I understand. The USA, always there when you need them, eventually.'

Moses wonders exactly what he has got himself into as Allen stands to toast the Americans and the poet Anthony but promptly collapses in front of Penne, and the bowl of red apples.

43
Death

The pain felt something like acid reflux, a sort of continuous, foul, hurting chest grip accompanied by a shortness of breath and fatigue. It was so intense that one could not count a thousand sheep, or in this case, goats. Allen loses consciousness and drifts to some place that is neither home nor his body. The last thing he can really discern is Bret approaching fast and Mateo exclaiming, 'Oh my god! Should I call Father Thyme or the Doctor?'

To the sound of "Rock the Casbah", a fine song by the Clash, Allen is in a space of his own. He can see from below Penne crying over him, Bret banging hard, very, hard on his chest. He knows the gardener's going to bust his ribs at that rate, but he no longer feels any pain. Saffy attempts a kiss of life as "Sharif don't like it" rings over his temples, the Windy Bar, and the people assembled providing relief. They all hear, "It's cool to dig this chanting thing". But as the crowd below catches a whiff of that crazy Casbah jive, and to the words "Sharif don't like it", Allen dies.

Unlike that other glorious song, Allen is pleasantly surprised to find that there is, in fact, no stairway to heaven. He is most fortunate as all that climbing might have given him a heart attack. What there is appears to be a vast tunnel of weightless bathing light that fluoresces so very bright in ever-changing pastel hues. A pathway, yes, but with no signs, and it all seems to weave together around him like dancing crystal stars leading him one way. Up. The only way is up. With every step forward, the light becomes distinctly brighter and appears to emanate from a single, mighty source. The air is sweet with cinnamon, or vanilla, but definitely not Anthony's ouzo. Snippets of indistinguishable languages can be overheard drifting lazily in, and then out, of earshot. It is all indiscernible. The light radiates through a large pair of ornate, distinctly old iron gates topped by scrollwork that looks almost Hebrew, with gilded Roman finials and Islamic crescent moons. Judging by their appearance, the gates look to have recently been painted in pink and white with a hint of pearl. *I bet that paint job cost a bit.* A large note is taped to the right gate post. It reads "Caution - Wet Paint".

There is a large black angel with a huge pair of angel wings, spread out, wearing a kind of white, off-the-shoulder—or off-the-wing—toga. *That must be Saint Peter*, thinks Allen. *Shit! Am I fucking dead?* There appears to be a small queue at the gate. Saint Peter has a clipboard and a feather quill, presumably self-grown. Allen is slightly bemused. *So, they recycle up here too, that's nice.* To the left of the gate is a small, double-stacked, portacabin office. The two-storey structure is held together with scaffolding and all painted in pearl. Another sign in brass, like a business registration plate, is brightly polished and screwed to the door. Allen reckons it reads "No Entry to the General Public". There is also a multi-language board to the side of the door which reads, in English first, "Thank You for your Patience. Death is the price of Love and Love is the price of Patience".

There is an elderly couple being attended to. Their grey hair blows wild and free in the slight breeze. They appear, from Allen's viewpoint, to be getting physically younger by the second, to the point where somewhere at early middle age, Saint Peter raises his hand and shouts authoritatively 'Enough!' and their age instantly stabilises.

Next in line is a family of Japanese taking photos on a Nikon camera with a huge zoom lens. Allen realises they struggle, mainly due to the obvious impediment that the mother has only one arm, which is still freshly bandaged and connected to a cannula. The dad, who looks equally injured, is naked to the chest and his midriff is heavily patched. The kids, a boy and a girl, are injured too. Allen is certain he recognises the dad, but he just can't seem to place him. Not surprising under the circumstances, but the family seems so grateful when Allen offers to take a photo of them. He grips the camera, finds the viewfinder and the shutter button, and adds 'Say cheese or Chizu.' They all smile at his poor attempt at their home language.

'Sorry we all look so messed up,' admits the father. 'There was a road accident on the Shuto Expressway just before Tokyo. The kids went through the front window and we got trapped when a Nissan transporter decided to drop a couple of its vehicles on and in front of us. It made global headlines, I believe.'

'Shit, buddy, that's truly awful! Not the headlines, but the accident!' Allen points to his chest. 'Heart attack for me, I think.' He strokes his chin. 'You know, I'm sure I recognise you from somewhere, man, a hotel maybe? Athens perhaps?'

The father looks worried now, which really, on judgment day, should be the last of his concerns.

'That's it!' Allen's memory finally kicking in, 'the Hotel Apollo Amore, you met my future fiancée there. She called you rather uncharitably Tuna Guy, sorry for that.'

'No matter,' adds Mr Tuna looking at his wife, who appears not to have heard and is trying to take a picture of Saint Peter with his clip board. 'But please say no more!'

44
Check-in

The Japanese family is all processed and checked in. Saint Peter ticks them off his itinerary, just like Allen used to do, and hands the one-armed mum some leaflets entitled "Welcome to Heaven" with the strapline "All you need to know about the afterlife and more". She grasps them rather awkwardly with her good arm.

'I suggest you all go to Health and Healing first,' Saint Peter advises. 'I'm just Reception, Direction and Age Adjustment. Keep going straight on, and turn left and it's the first building on the right, immediately next to another big pair of locked red gates. Not Bill's Gates,' he jokes badly. 'They're clearly identified by a large sign that reads "The Other Place", you can't miss them. Gabriel's shitty sense of humour, I'm afraid. Just don't cock up and try to go through them, that's the only departure point from here. It is slightly warmer on the other side of that gate, though, but very noisy. They do make surprisingly good toasties however. Next!'

Allen realises that means him.

'And who are you exactly?' Asks the Angel, flapping a wing and looking at his list and then back at Allen. A couple of pure black feathers drop to the ground. 'Bugger,' grunts Saint Peter. 'Moulting again.'

'Allen, to answer your question.'

'Allen what?' Peter requests, sounding a tad tetchy as only the finest administrators can.

'Allen Freeman.'

'You're that DJ, are you not, Fluff guy? You ain't down on my list yet.'

'No, I'm not a DJ, I'm a tour rep… or was…' Allen replies. 'And my name is spelt with two Ls and an E. My middle name is also Mason and not Leslie, therefore I'm not called Fluff and not losing any, unlike you.'

'I'm telling you, don't get fresh with me, son, I'm the brother with the wings. Age-wise, I pre-date you by thousands of years, yet still have a better haircut. Anyway, moving on. There must be an admin fuck up. Hold your horses, and not the four from the apocalypse,' he laughs. 'I need to get the boss.'

'And who is the boss exactly?' Asks Allen. 'I ain't happy, you know!'

'Dead people rarely are,' Peter replies with heavy irony. 'But don't get cocky with me, son. I'll get the big J. I think he's taking a nap in the office.'

Saint Peter shuts the gate with a Samsung remote, leaving Allen outside, feeling pissed off, vulnerable, and very confused.

Big J arrives with Saint Peter and his clipboard. 'Allen,' indicates Peter, pointing at the tour rep through the gate. Big J is not what Allen expected. Jesus is in fact a rather short, and somewhat paunchy, fellow with an old dad beer belly. He rubs the sleep from his truly hypnotising blue eyes.

'Sorry Allen, it's been exceptionally busy around here lately, what with another sodding war and loads of fucking dead. It's hard to work out which ones are the bad guys.'

He is wearing a yellow hard hat with fairy lights around it. Some are not functioning and others are irritatingly flashing. The hard hat has JCB on it. Jesus spots Allen looking at his hat.

'Ah! Another joke by that twat Gabriel. I dig the halo, but the batteries need replacing. The JCB joke is crap, but we do have a digger or two of theirs up here. It should read JBC, Jesus Before Christ, but I think Gabriel suffers with dyslexia.' To complement the yellow helmet, he is wearing a full-length orange robe. 'It's Buddhist Week, right?' Jesus asks, turning to Peter. 'I'm correct am I not? It's still on?'

Saint Peter nods his head in accent.

'Cool, and thank the Lord for that. Well, thank me, really.' The Lord turns to Allen. 'I bet you'd like that, dear man, all that reincarnation stuff, some finger cymbals, the odd bongo, and plenty of chanting? Its real fun!'

'I would prefer cardiopulmonary resuscitation rather than reincarnation.'

'See, I told you he was a cheeky chappie,' Peter says, preening his wings.

'Will you just stop that, please, you know it irritates me! It's like I come out here and start scratching my balls.'

'Sorry boss.' Peter apologies and furls up his wings.

Dry ice drifts over and seeps peacefully through Heaven's gates. It twirls to some distant music that sounds suspiciously like "I Want to Break Free". *God knows I want to break free!*

'But he can't.' Grunts the big J as a truly ear-piercing screech rises above saint Mercury's song. It sounds to Allen as almost three octaves higher than normal. As if the voice has been inhaling helium. He wonders if they have balloons up here. The shriek comes again, this time more recognisable. It floats on the slight breeze with all the other poor tour rep's nightmares.

'Alleeeeeeen! It's gwate up here, but mi dimmer switch is broken and Peter's maintenance guys are shite. They know loads about religious stuff but diddly zilch, nothing, about electrics!'

Allen collapses for a second time that day outside the Pearly Gates, this time from a full-blown panic attack.

'Get him a Tango.'

'I don't think he's up to dancing yet,' adds Saint Peter to Big J. He looks at the collapsed Allen through the gated bars.

'No, the sodding drink, you stupid bird man, and no vodka in it. And before you ask, I know where you keep your stash, in that chrome filing cabinet, good job it's Absolut, I won't need to give you absolution.'

'Right away boss!' Peter adds, heading back to the portacabin and its retro pink fridge-freezer, then returning quickly. 'We're clean out of Tango, boss, so I made him freshly-squeezed orange juice, vitamin C and all.'

'He's a bleeding dead man, what the fuck good do you think vitamin C is going to do?' Big J hands the juice to the still-gasping Allen through the railings.

'Jesus Christ!' Allen shouts upon hearing the approaching squeal from Grace Holy Houseman-Smith.

'What?' Jesus asks.

'Sorry JC, not you,' apologises Allen.

'Don't take my word in vain, son.' Orders the Big J.

'No, seriously sorry, no offence meant.'

Allen peers through the fence. *Sweet Jesus! Look it's her, that wretched woman, the Devil!*

'I see you fixed her leg! But this is torture, man, you sure I'm at the right gate?' Allen asks like he's at some airport check-in desk.

'In truth, Allen, and I always tell the truth as you well know, I'm not sure at all, which is why I'm here to sort this king cock up out.'

Grace is advancing rapidly. She appears to have a handsome bearded guy with her and two small, blonde-haired kids, who must be twins, seven years of age, each with a set of little wings.

Allen looks at the Big J straight on through the closed gates into those big, blue, compassionate eyes.

'Buddy, I need to see your Dad, and straight away. No excuses, the Almighty Jehovah, the Master of Creation, the Big Kahuna.'

45
ELECTRICS AND THE ALMIGHTY

Grace is now at the gates that keeps Allen and his orange juice out.

'You comin' in?' She asks. 'I want you to meet my babies, fix the dimmer switch and say hi to my fine friend here,' whom she looks adoringly at. 'His name's Eugenios of Trebizond, he was huge in the fourth century, a martyrdom thing, but since Jesus fixed him up, he's sodding ace in bed. We call him ET for short or just U-Genius.'

'That's nice.' Allen says. 'I'm glad you've finally found your kids and sexual happiness. Not sure what's going on with me though, I'm still waiting to find out. May take a while for the switch. Hello kids!' He waves at them. 'Having fun? Cool wings, do they work?'

'Jesus fixed the kids' age at seven for me. They can do that up here, don't ya know? Age Adjustment Department, I think that's wot the gaff is called. The kids were Christian's, our twins that we lost prematurely and yeah, the fuckers are flying around all over the place. They're a bit like pet owls, bless em.'

Jesus arrives in a golf cart. 'It's actually the Pope Mobile,' he announces, pointing to the vehicle. 'Had the apostle Paul salvage it for me, he was a car dealer as well as a tent-maker. It's a really nifty piece of gear, power-steering and bulletproof windows, not that we need them up here. Ready to go, Allen?'

'Where?' Allen asks nervously.

'To meet your maker, the supreme being,' the Big J replies with a grin. 'Although you may be surprised with what you find.'

Peter opens the gates and Allen hops on board.

'It won't take too long but the journey is all uphill, a bit like life really,' he comments, sucking on a humbug. 'Want one?' They're in the glove compartment, help yourself.'

Allen does just that. 'I've not had one of these in years. Since I was a child in fact. It's strange how they taste the same as I remember.'

'I know, in both departments.'

Allen looks at the winding road before them and the vegetation on either side. Exotic plants, not a Hellebore in sight, just huge apple trees full of the red fruit, tropical palms, arum lilies, sun flowers, lupins, red anthuriums, hydrangeas, all seemingly, and perpetually, flowering at the same time on the verges of the winding yellow stone road.

'We travel on a yellow brick road?' Allen asks.

Yep. Old Frank Baum, the author of Oz, sort of knew his stuff. Although we ain't got a tin man without a heart up here.'

The road leads to an establishment that looks strangely like a Travelodge. Jesus parks up in a disability space.

'No one will know,' he tells Allen, doing a hand break turn which would have earned a worthy appraisal from Jeremy Clarkson. 'Besides, I've got a permit.'

'Are you joining me, dear Lord?' Allen asks.

'No, man, this is for you to do alone, so to speak. Go through the glass doors and head immediately right to the reception desk, you are expected so don't worry.'

Allen gets off the Pope mobile, his feet crunching on the yellow gravel. It looks like Yorkshire Cream Stone.

'Through the doors and to the right,' repeats Allen in a murmur. He arrives at the reception desk. The receptionist, a kind dark-haired lady with huge pink fingernails, looks up from her book. Allen notes the title, *Creating with Batik*.

'Ah, you must be Allen!' She comments kindly. 'The tour rep? You are expected. Please sign the register.'

'And who are you?'

'Mary,' she replies.

'What, Baby Jesus's mum?'

'Well, yes and, as you know, he is not a baby at all. But it's all rather complicated. Wear these.' She hands him a pair of shades with tinted sides which would have done Stevie Wonder proud. 'But not until you go in as you won't be able to see and may injure yourself further, existing heart problems and all.' Allen takes the glasses. 'It's the Conference Room, second door on the left just past the lift. Knock, put your glasses on, then enter. Oh and there is a fine for the non-return of the glasses.'

46
The supreme being

A large pair of Mahogany doors confront him with equally large gold knobs and a modest sign, also in gold, that reads "Conference Room". He thinks he can hear some ethereal music behind the closed doors. He fits his glasses, adjusts them, and realises he can see absolutely nothing at all, but he keeps them on, knocks and enters.

'"Ray of Light" by someone called Madonna. She hasn't released this yet but the song is set firmly in her young head,' says a charming voice.

Even through the glasses, the light within the room is so immense it folds and weaves and bursts in strangely cool minor sun blasts or explosions without the noise, chaos, and mess. It is like being inside a live kaleidoscope.

'Are you the Supreme Being, the one and only? And I don't mean Elvis. Are you the Great Creator?' Allen asks to the floating mass of light.

'Yes, of course! You sound surprised, Allen, why?'

'I just kind of thought the Architect of the Universe would be some dude with a long white beard, a bit like Father Christmas. Someone who could make all bad right and who wears a big cream frock.'

'Ah, the usual preconceptions!' The spinning voice replies. 'And yes, but by your tone and, surprisingly for you, I am in fact a woman. I cannot make all the injustice right, however, but I am the Mother of all Creation. This confusion really pisses me off sometimes, especially when Saint Nic is up here doing his Christmas thing.'

She pauses the conversation. Now hovering over her chair, she extends a golden hand to scoop up some honey-roasted pistachios from an old bowl on the table. A simple terracotta pot that appears, as per Allen's imagination, to resemble the Holy Grail.

'Nuts?' She asks between munches. Reading Allen's mind, she states. 'Yep, the very same. Sir Galahad bought it back from the Holy

Land. He still argues with Sir Bors de Ganis and Sir Percival over who found the sodding thing. Rather pleasing piece, though, but I digress.'

Allen then kindly shakes his head.

'I know more than you know. However, without getting on to quantum physics, even I do not know it all, unfortunately. Your big questions are still my big questions, darling. Who made me, who made you and why, how vast is space and time itself? But here, right now, dear man, you need to listen as this is important.'

Allen shifts uneasily in his chair as a further ray of light from the Mother of Creation is penetrating his sunglasses.

'We are all branches of the same tree and that tree is life itself. The Hindus have Brahman, not the wonder bra, the Buddhists have Vishnu, Islam has Prophet Muhammad, the Jews Abraham, Shintos have the sun goddess Amaterasu, the Taoists have Lao Tzu, the Protestants, Methodists and the Catholics have Jesus, but still argue, and the Druids have whoever they want. But my point is, they are all my sons and daughters. Even dear Lucifer, who has a tough job down there. So many evil souls to process and punish, and not just from your galaxy, but he remains one of my own. We meet once a year at All Hallows Eve, or Halloween as the Americans call it. But enough of theology, I must explain something before we begin.'

'Begin what?' Allen asks, bemused.

'Begin a basic understanding,' advises the Mother of all Creation, changing to a relaxing shade of vivid green. 'Look at your watch. It is not waterproof, right, and yet you have jumped into that pool to save a poet and it still works, does it not?' Allen looks at his Minnie Mouse watch that his dearest Penne bought him as a joke in Athens.

'That primitive machine of yours still works, even though it shouldn't. It still reads time. Now look at its hands. It has an hour hand, a minute hand. And a third hand. Do they not also work?'

'Yes, the watch works, so what?'

'Well look again.'

Allen looks again and, yes, the hands on the watch go round, but appear to take two steps forward and then two steps back. 'Do you understand yet?' Asks the Creator. 'It's called relativity. The relativity or even "relevance" of time. Time does not progress here, it starts where it stops and stops where it starts. Everything here is floating in a state of perpetual suspense. The concept of time as you know it does not exist here. I believe Einstein nearly got it right.'

The Mother of all Creation waves a hand from the vivid green and a vision appears as if by magic on the table before him. It blurs at first, but then becalms into something like a crystal-clear pool, a porthole to another place or time. Allen realises he is looking at a picture of himself, lying prone on a gurney. He always thought the name had something to do with the Channel Islands back home. He is surrounded by paramedics with electrics, his dear Penne holding his hand, in tears, Saffron, also in tears, clinging to Kevin and Bret. Anthony stares at him with profound sadness in his creative eyes, and Mateo is offering free drinks that even the poet declines.

'Must be serious…' Allen suggests rather flippantly from his astral viewpoint.

'Now look further. Look at the poet, read his words.' The divine being suggests.

Allen looks at Anthony's manuscript that lays flat but sodden on his lap in the chair with the faulty brake. He can read its title, he can comprehend the strangely scrawled words accompanied by many curious doodles.

The Architect

Such perfect, perfect symmetry,
said the architect to me,
whilst I drifted on a cold black couch
of paper-wrapped melamine.
I believe I spoke at some length to the architect,
as the medicated mix surfed another vein.
Was it a mere moment,
when the monitor's green trace ran flat,
unable to ride the wave.
How do we sustain this balance then?
Said the architect to me.
An equilibrium,
of such delicate grace,
on a tide that will ebb and flow.

As the beam tilts ever slightly
on the brass scale
that hangs below,
in that sterile place.

We spin in one direction,
said the architect to me.
And it appears that you still slowly turn,
on a fulcrum held by a thread.
Look, it pivots still,
watch its slow glide, its ups and downs,
an imbalance, indecision at its worst.
However, your bed here remains unmade,
a home for you is neither drawn, nor built,
for you are not yet dead.

Look.

'Do you understand now?' Asks the Mother of all Creation. 'You are an intelligent man and, surely, must have a vague comprehension of time by now. Down there you are dead, but only for a mere dragon's breath. Fifteen minutes or so, whereas up here you are alive and have been, for what must seem like ages.'

'Was that a Bruce Lee film?' Allen asks.

'Don't be flippant with me, son. Wrath of God and all…'

Allen looks again at the face before him on the conference table screen, wondering if it is something new made by Sony. He observes the paramedics, one looks quite hot in a sexy way. He watches as Sexy takes out the defibrillator from its orange portable charging case while the Mother of Creation slides a clipped file of papers from one end of the conference table to Allen. The papers skim over the image and the highly-polished wood, but the picture remains as before, almost paused.

'What is this?' He picks up the document.

'Read it.'

Allen opens the dossier. It states in bold caps "Confidentiality Agreement". She rolls him a solid gold cross pen.

'Harvey Nics', it was in the summer sale.'

Allen skips to the last page like a true professional. She has already signed, Allen observes and notes the witness, Jesus, not a Jehovah's Witness.

'Jesus can sort that later, but you need to sign now, please.'

He makes his mark above his name. Allen Mason Freeman.

'You are now a free man, and thankfully not a Mason. And this,' admits Mother pointing to the document, 'this after-world legal balls thing that you have just signed is our standard confidentiality agreement. Any breeches to it will necessitate my further involvement. However, it appears I owe you an apology. A king cock up of certainly biblical proportions has been made here, which is not of your making. And, as the poet says, your time is certainly not yet due. So, providing you stick to the terms and conditions, I will not see you again for about thirty of your earthly years. Now watch the image. You may feel a slight discomfort. I will see you later, much, much later. And have fun! Always remember, communists want something for nothing, and capitalists want everything for something.'

Allen watches Sexy charge the defibrillators, Penne now cries uncontrollably as she is led away by another paramedic who vaguely resembles the great Kenny Rogers. Sexy positions the monitor on one of Mateo's dining tables still bearing the printed paper map of Kea which the goats missed in their assault on the Windy Bar. Her other assistant, a bearded fellow, cuts up the front of Allen's Prada tee-shirt to expose his hairless chest. Allen rolls his eyes.

'There was no need for that.' He thinks out loud. 'I suppose I could turn it into a waistcoat, maybe a cardigan.'

The charges are placed and he hears someone shout, 'Clear!' They zap to his chest cavity but the green monitor still rides flat.

'Again,' orders Sexy, injecting him with some stuff.

'Ouch, that was sharp!' Allen grunts, not knowing whether his words are heard down there or up here, wherever he is.

'Another, and now,' shouts the lovely Sexy. Bang, the secondary charge hits dangerously close to Allen's nipples. *Decision time*, thinks Allen as Penne, who appears to have escaped from her guardian, hits Allen very hard on his chest.

'Don't you die on me you fucking bastard!' She screams. Everyone else involved watches the monitor like an England football World Cup qualifier, a real nail-biter that lasts for what seems, and usually is, an age.

The monitor's trace still runs a flat line. A divine, cooling breeze blows across the Windy Bar and a host of small blue butterflies appear over Allen. As if by magic, the machine bibs a single beautiful note. The beat starts to pulse stronger for all to view, followed by a regular rhythm.

Ah shit! Forgot to fix Grace's wretched dimmer switch!

Allen splutters back to life on the medics' gurney.

'Fuck, that was weird, but stick to the plan with Diazepam! And where's the poet?'

The end … or not

Grasp a stone that is truly, very hard like granite, an Obsidian, or an ancient Celtic hag stone. Hold it, then turn it in your palm. Wonder where its age emanates from and how the human condition may be just the same, albeit more transient, yet still a substance that lasts longer than soapstone or sandstone, which can be washed away at any given time. But not a free, living soul, which surely remains as lasting as the rock you hold in your hand and as lasting as perhaps eternity itself. Find your rock and you find immortality.

Epilogue

The Crawfords' exhibition is a great success. All the artwork has been professionally mounted and framed, with the notable exception of Denholm's engorged penile life drawing, which has been deemed unsuitable for display. Margaritte has even sold some paintings, and not just to the tourists. The Crawfords then departed the island happy with the cash from the exhibition sales, leaving the rest of the paintings on semi-permanent display in a gallery in Loulida, whose owner is a friend of Allen's and a resident of the capital city on the island.

Bret turns out to be much more than a first aider in the medical department and a gardener in foul Derbyshire. The news of his inheritance comes as some shock. He didn't even know he had a great aunt called Mary who had been living on a rambling estate near Crickhowell, in the southeastern Welsh countryside near Abergavenny, with a magnificent view of the Black Mountains. In her will, the estate and a substantial amount of cash had been left to Bret, with full instructions for him to maintain his aunt's glorious self-designed gardens. Upon viewing it, it became apparent that the whole place would require much attention in both the interior and exterior areas. Naturally, Bret invited his newfound friends—and apparently lovers, comrades in arms even, call it what you will—Kevin and Saffron, who accepted the invitation. The plan was to develop and explore Bret's idea to energise the grand Victorian house and gardens into a non-religious spa and safe, recluse resort. It remains transformed, without a hint of cult.

Christian, Grace's happily widowed husband, has moved to the hills on Kea and built a fine villa with a pool that seemed to hover to infinity, so well placed by the Athenian architect, out over the mountain and off into thin air. The panorama is spectacular and there isn't a dimmer switch in sight. His new venture, which combines boat trips and diving with tourist accommodation, is flourishing in conjunction with Yannis and Moses Jones' Scuba Diving School.

The Royal Marines, Finn and Alistair Thompson, have left as anonymously as they arrived: with no goodbyes, and leaving a considerable unpaid bar tab at Mateo's bar.

The orange-eared bastard of a cat was adopted by Penne and a reluctant Allen. Penne names him Brutus, after the Roman politician. Not that Brutus had orange ears. Allen continues to call it "the bastard cat", or "the feline beast". He retains his employment on fully-paid sick leave by his kind and gracious employers at Laskarina. A replacement tour rep arrived soon to fulfil his duties. To be fair, Allen milks his heart condition as the Athenian specialists can find nothing wrong with him. *Thank the Supreme Creator for that,* Allen thinks, remembering the Confidentiality Agreement he has signed.

Monty, Isabella and Ferdinand North the antique dealer visit Allen's apartment for vodka and lime's care of Russell the lemon tree.

'Don't tell the Social Services that Mont is drinking vodka,' Isabella asks him whilst Ferdinand endeavours to find the bathroom, which really should not be that difficult considering there are only four rooms in the entire place. After a rather long, but not unnoticed, time, he struggles back onto the small balcony, delicately clutching Allen's bedside lamp. Allen assumes that Ferdinand has been taking a shit. *Always a bad party vibe at someone else's gaff.*

'Know what this is?' Ferdinand asks him, clearly excited.

'Our bedside lamp?' Allen answers, whilst Penne endeavours to steal another one of Russell's unripe lemons to pretend it is a lime, for a further round of drinks.

'It's a 1931 René Lalique, blue Six Danseuses lamp worth about eighteen thousand US dollars, maybe more at auction. It's extremely rare to find one this perfect!'

'Fuck!' Allen thinks back to the great sex with Penne and the near-busted light fitting. 'Sorry Monty, but fuck, fuck, diddly fuck! That's worth more than my pension! What's the value in pounds?'

Ferdinand does the calculation. 'Well... give or take a few quid, and depending on...'

'Get to the point.' Isabella North interjects, obviously too familiar with her husband's calculus.

'On current exchange rates,' he continues, 'about thirteen

thousand pounds sterling.'

'What?' Penne splutters. 'For the bedroom lamp? Have we got anymore, Allen?'

'If you wish,' continues the antique dealer, 'I will take this masterpiece of glass and sell it for you, possibly at Christie's. Minus their and my commission, you will make a fine sum.'

December on Kea turns out to be absolutely great. Penne decides ballet and pole dancing are no longer for her. She and Allen marry. The ceremony is conducted by Father Thyme, with a little help from Father Basil. They have an unusual wedding march, "Mr Loverman", by the one and only Shabba Ranks. The newly-weds move out of the bakery flat, taking Russell the lemon tree and Brutus the orange-eared cat to a semi-derelict villa with outbuildings suitable for conversion. Allen resigns his position at Laskarina after receiving the handsome bank transfer from North Antiques. The lamp did better at auction than expected and was bought by an American. Allen received a total of fourteen thousand five hundred and ninety pounds.

It is a Saturday, Penne and Allen are sitting on wooden packing cases on the terrace, drinking red wine and eating fresh bread with a light marinade and olives and herb grilled chicken, all dangerously positioned on a makeshift worm-eaten table covered with a pristine white tablecloth. Allen is the first to see the white FedEx van driving up the private potholed stone road that leads to their villa. It approaches at great speed, shrouded in clouds of dust.

'Company, hon.'

'It's the sofa I ordered.' Penne replies.

The van skids to a halt, spraying dust over their food. The FedEx man exits the transit and opens the rear doors.

'It's heavy!' He says.

'Well, it is a sofa!' Penne adds.

'Small sofa! Unless you have a load of very tiny people living here!' He hands over the heavy package, no bigger than half a shoe box. 'Enjoy,' he adds, then leaves.

Allen looks at Penne, Penne looks at Allen, then they both look at the box.

'Are you going to open it then?' She asks.

Allen rips clear the wide tape seals that caution "With Care, Heavy", to discover a wooden case sealed with nails beneath the corrugated card.

'I'll need a hammer to prise open the lid.'

He returns with a claw hammer whilst Penne surveys the box suspiciously, sipping on the wine. Allen prises off the pine lid to find a postcard. The postcard, slightly faded and very dog-eared, depicts an image of the Lion of Kea. He shows it to Penne.

'Well, what does it say?'

Allen turns it over.

'"We never forget our friends. Please settle our drinks bill at Mateo's out of this. Regards, AFT."'

'It's from the bloody marines!' He exclaims.

'What else is in there then?'

Allen peels away the layered, shredded card packer to find three weighty small brick-sized objects, neatly wrapped in brown paper. He rips at one and the sun blasts off the exposed block. A blistering light glows on the solid gold ingot stamped with a menacing iron cross surmounted by a clutching imperial German eagle. A note states its current market value: roughly fifty thousand pounds each. One hundred and fifty thousand pounds worth of gold sit in Allen's lap.

'Fuck! Thank you Lord! No need to invent those air-filled flip flops now, even though I was going to call them Jesus Air-souls!'

'Don't you mean assholes?' Penne added helpfully.

'No, hon. Sandals with the strapline "Walk on Water, the Jesus Way!".'

Jesus, Mother of all creation, fuck! My sweet Holy Lord!

Yep! The real end.
Or is it the beginning?

ACKNOWLEDGEMENTS

One may be full of words but they do not necessarily all fall within their righteous place. With my editor Chloe Slann, they most gloriously always do. My heartfelt thanks. Allen and James could not have achieved this without Alicia Violet's calming purple imagery and her tireless pursuit to keep the author in check.

Credits: Pyper Egerton

Born in Birmingham in 1961 but now residing in Cornwall, James is a father to one, a second father to two, a grandfather to five, and a devoted husband to one.

In his early years, James gained a scholarship to attend Worksop College in Nottinghamshire, where he dedicated his studies to the arts. He then trained to be a designer at Matthew Bolton College, in Birmingham, before joining Mastrom Limited, his father's lithographic print company. Many years later, the challenges of digitlal printing forced him to reconsider his career path.

James has always had a passion for literature, art, and music, which he immensely incorporates into his life, believing wholeheartedly in their therapeutic benefits for the soul. Among other achievements and commitments, James played drums for the eighties' band Whizz for Atoms, which reached number twenty in the French singles charts.

As an artist, James regards his art as being vaguely offensive and often politically incorrect.

So groove on!